EMBER FURY

cathy brett

Cathy Brett has been scribbling stuff for more than twenty years; as a fashion illustrator, as a jet-setting spotter of global trends and as a consultant to the behemoths of the British high street.

She now lectures in design and unashamedly plunders her students' lives for sensational storylines and characters.

EMBER FURY

cathy brett

headline

First published in Great Britain in 2009 by
HEADLINE PUBLISHING GROUP

1

Cataloguing in Publication Data is available from the British Library

ISBN 978 0 7553 4788 9

Typeset by Jason Cox

Printed and bound in Great Britain by
Clays Ltd, St Ives plc

Headline's policy is to use papers that are natural, renewable and recyclable products and
made from wood grown in sustainable forests. The logging and manufacturing processes
are expected to conform to the environmental regulations of the country of origin.

HEADLINE PUBLISHING GROUP
An Hachette UK Company
338 Euston Road
London NW1 3BH

www.headline.co.uk
www.hachette.co.uk

For Daisy and Mia

To my sister, Nicola, to my mum and dad, to Grace and Rachel and to the students at UCA Epsom (whom I've drawn, with and without their knowledge),

Ta very much.

Fizzzzz. . . crack. . . whoosh. . .

It was a tiny tongue at first, then it spread like a rippling, orange blanket over the floorboards and poured itself up the walls. My heart was pounding and there was a kinda buzzing in my head. I couldn't breathe. I couldn't move. Then I gasped.

'Cool!'

'Hey! What are you doing? You stupid. . .'

Finn grabbed my arm and I lost the rest of what he said in a blast of pain as my forehead slammed against the door frame and he yanked me outside into the darkness. He opened the car door and shoved me inside.

I was still watching the flames. They'd already reached the second cabin of the motel and had started to tickle the roof. Then the building sneezed, an exploding, pyrotechnic sneeze. Fountains of window glass showering down on to the ground.

'Let's get out of here!'

We'd not driven far when the accident happened. I saw the rabbit sitting in the middle of the road and jerked the wheel.

The car swerved and we flew into a ditch.

Within seconds, the police cars were everywhere, lights flashing. They put us both in handcuffs. Can you believe it? Finn wouldn't even look at me in the back of the cop car. I could see he was really angry but scared, too. He said, 'I told you this would happen. Didn't I tell you? You wouldn't listen, you crazy kid.'

That felt like a punch in the stomach. It hurt more than the gash on my head or the bruise on my shoulder that I got in the crash. I hated him! Not just because he called me a kid, but for loads of other reasons. I'd been so dumb. What an idiot! Stupid, stupid!

My shoulder really hurt, but not as much as the place in my chest where my heart used to be. It had been ripped out and was lying there on the desk in the police station, oozy and bloody. A lady cop, who looked really bored and fed up, had taken the handcuffs off, but you could tell from her face that she was thinking that it was a mistake because she was scowling as if I was some serial killer, a terrorist or a psychopath or something. To be honest, I wouldn't have had the energy to be a psychopath, I was so tired. Every time I moved it was like swimming through hot fudge sauce. If I'd tried to grab her gun – you know, like desperate, wild-eyed prisoners do sometimes in the movies – she'd have slammed me to the floor in an armlock before I could have taken a breath.

We were waiting for the other cop, the one with a big belly, who was calling my dad in Los Angeles. The door opened and big-belly cop walked in carrying a yellow notepad which he put down on the table. . . next to my oozing heart.

'Well, young lady, it appears you were telling the truth,' he said and looked at the lady cop. 'Hey, Betty. We've got us a gen-u-ine celebrity!'

'You don't say,' Betty replied, sneering.

Wait. You're thinking, hold it, pause, scroll back! I should start at the beginning. The beginning of the story. Fill you in on a few things. So, this is the bit where the screen goes wobbly to tell you there's a flashback coming. . .

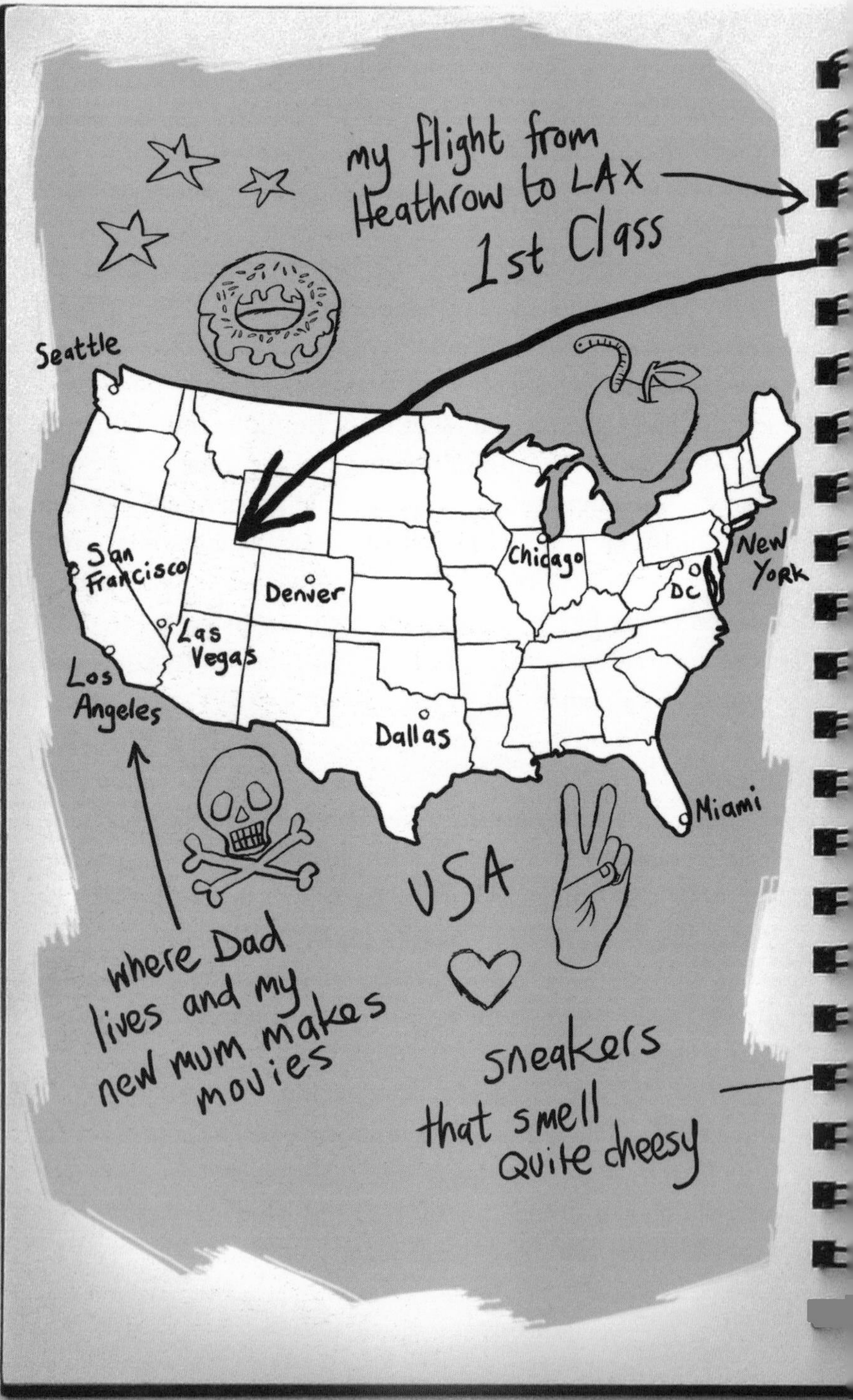
my flight from
Heathrow to LAX
1st Class
Seattle
San
Francisco
Denver
Las
Vegas
Los
Angeles
Dallas
Chicago
New
York
DC
Miami
USA
where Dad
lives and my
new mum makes
movies
sneakers
that smell
quite cheesy

Episode One

First Class Boredom, Men in Dark Suits and My Malibu Nightmare

INT. JET AIRLINER, MID-ATLANTIC — NIGHT. The luxurious first class cabin is in almost total darkness. A narrow column of light pours down on to a window seat and a pile of very messy, bright, red hair, under a blue blanket. The redhead is reading.

VOICE OVER: That's me, three weeks earlier, so-called 'delinquent teenager', Ember Fury. It's Em for short and Ember Abigail Morton-Fury for long. Mum said she named me Ember when I popped out of her with all that bright orange hair. That's my real mum Amica Morton, not my new mum, Charity Lane. And yes, I do mean Charity Lane, the Hollywood actress. Charity is Dad's second wife and she's only ten years older than me. What a cliché, huh? They moved into a house in Los Angeles a few months ago, so that's why I'm in a jet, on my way from London to LAX to stay with them for the summer holidays. . . maybe longer. I visit my dad during every school break, in lots of different places,

wherever he happens to be touring. Well, when I say 'visit my dad' I mean his people, his entourage. Dad doesn't really do 'the dad thing'.

I don't remember my dad being around much when I was small, but when he was, he always seemed to be unpacking or packing for the next tour. He used to make jokes all the time about needing to take parenting classes because he didn't have a clue about raising kids, but my mum said that just being around when I was growing up would have helped. Me and Mum became kinda self-contained and learned not to need him, until Mum got sick. Dad was the one who paid the bills and bought us lots of fancy stuff, but I guess that's not enough, is it?

The air steward handed me a pillow and I put my book down.

'Can I get you anything else, miss?'

'Vodka rocks,' I said with a grin. He didn't smile back.

'Yeah, right. Nice try,' he said, and returned to the front of the plane and disappeared behind a curtain.

'Fathead!' I whispered, and picked up my book again. The man across the aisle glanced at me. 'What are you looking at?' I asked. He shook his head and made a tsk sound. I wriggled about a bit, trying to get more comfortable, then squished the pillow up round my head and half closed my eyes.

Almost everyone was sleeping, some with those dumb eye shade things on, so that people know not to disturb them. The whole plane was really dark and kinda creepy, with a few kinda slashes of light piercing open paperback books and bouncing off the shiny head of the tutting guy across the aisle. There was a spooky, ghostly, swirling shape floating in front of him – the screen saver on his laptop. I couldn't get comfortable and I couldn't sleep. It was the noise. I was thinking, how could all these people sleep through it? Even when I put my hands over my ears I could feel the low growl of the engines. I didn't really want to watch another movie on the mini-screen that folded out from the seat in front and reading was giving me a headache, so I put in the earphones of my MP3 and selected 'most played' on shuffle.

As the band started playing inside my head, I looked over at the screen saver. Was it clouds or water? Maybe sand blowing across a desert? The sand became leaves and the leaves became rippling grass. The grass was a football pitch. Beckham's foot struck the ball and it sailed, in slow motion, into the corner of the net. The crowd roared. The goalkeeper trotted over, reached down and picked it up but it wasn't a ball any more. It was a white rabbit, nose twitching. The rabbit kicked its back legs, in a panic to escape, and the goalie dropped it. It hopped twice then disappeared down a hole.

I suppose I should give you a bit more info. You would have seen the pictures of the wedding on the Internet and in the gossip mags. Don't say you didn't see them because I know you did. The designer dress, the celebrity guest list, the paparazzi. So boring! Then Charity flew off to shoot some lame sci-fi movie in New Zealand, or somewhere like that, and my dad went straight to New York to finish the tour with his band. I went back to school. About a month later, I got an e-mail saying I could come and visit their new house in Malibu at the end of term. Then, I suppose, because of the 'thing' I did (which you also saw in the news), my end of term was a bit earlier than expected. Oh, by the way, I guess you know that my dad is Lyndon Fury, the lead singer with Slap! I know, I know! Rock star dad, dead mother, actress stepmum, I've got to be a mixed-up kid, right?

MRS FURY

Starlet Charity
marries Slap!
frontman.

...Fury, 44, is almost
...wice the age of his
...w bride. Cont. p18-25

ARTIST WIFE SUFFERING FROM DEPRESSION SAYS SINGER

ROCK STAR DAUG...

STARS OF MUSIC & ART SAY GOODBYE TO AMICA

Politicians joined painters and popstars in London today at the funeral of tragic artist and rock star wife, Amica...

FORGET ME NOT

You might think you know me, but you don't. Don't believe everything you read in those celebrity magazines. They tell lies and invent sensational, malicious stuff that isn't true - especially when my mum died. They don't know what it's really like being me. All those stories about me stealing stuff, getting drunk, being expelled from exclusive schools, burning a couple of them down - well, only some of that actually happened. I'm not a 'wild child' and I'm not an 'out-of-control rich brat'. OK? Everyone thinks I'm spoilt. You know, 'why is she such a bad kid when she had all that advantage?' But I didn't ask for the money and big houses and posh schools and all that. I just wanted a nice, normal home and a nice, normal family, but it didn't work out that way.

When I was little, about six or seven I think, I picked
up a really pretty box of matches in a café in France. I
liked how it rattled and carried it around in my pocket. The
box was red, white and blue, quite 60s retro, with a sort of
target on it and the words 'light my fire' on the side.
It was the first box in my collection.

Mum got sick soon after that. I
think I always knew she might die
because everyone started talking
about what would happen to me if
she wasn't around, like when she was
in hospital and all that. I wanted
to go with her, and when
they said I couldn't. . . I
set fire to my bed.
I was nine and at
boarding school when
Mum died.

fire *noun* combustion, destructive
burning, flames, burning wood,
coal or other
fire alarm
fireball
firebomb
firebrigade
fire extinguisher

Pyromania means 'a mental derangement, excitement or excessive enthusiasm for fire'. That's what Dr Redmond at Orchard Farm said. The police called it arson - 'malicious setting on fire of house or other property'.

STAR FURY DEFENDS 'CONFUSED' DAUGHTER

EXT. LAX — DAY. CLOSE-UP: EMBER FURY, glass doors closing behind her, is screwing up her eyes in the bright California sunshine. An enormous silver 4x4 with blacked-out windows pulls up at the kerb. Two men in dark suits and matching shades leap out. One grabs her bags and the other opens the rear door.

I was quite annoyed that Dad wasn't at the airport to meet me. I peered into the gloom of the back seat. It was empty apart from a pair of enormous sunglasses on a stick – Charity Lane.

'Hey, Em!' she said, wrapping her skinny arms round me in an awkward hug. I was thrown back into the seat as the car pulled away, tyres squealing, at the speed of light.

'How was the flight? Your dad hoped you wouldn't mind, but he flew to San Francisco this morning for a couple of days. Are you OK?' she said and frowned at me, trying to be all concerned and empathetic.

I had resolved not to discuss my 'break' (that's what I'm going to call it for now), but just that one, simple, stupid question from my new stepmother made me think about my friends at the Farm and how much I missed them. I couldn't help it.

'Fine and fine,' I said, and rubbed a bit of water from under my eye.

'Hey, don't cry, sweetie,' she said, looking a bit worried.

'Oh, shuuuut uuuup!' I said, angry with myself. 'The sun was in my eyes.'

This was a lie. It *was* a bit of a tear, but I didn't want her to think I was upset, so I was acting like I didn't care, as hard as I could. 'And don't call me sweetie,' I said. There was silence for a few embarrassing seconds that felt like about half a century.

'Dr Redmond says you're doing OK. She called yesterday, you know, gave your dad a report on your progress.' Charity stroked my arm like I was her pet dog or something. I hate it when people do that.

'Mmm,' I said, wishing she would change the subject. You see, after the 'thing' happened at school, I went to this place called Orchard Farm. I'd been there for eight weeks, with a load of other 'mixed-up' kids, and had to talk to dumb psychiatrists and do stupid stuff like 'cognitive behavioural therapy'. It's a long story and I'll tell you about it later.

A cloud of exhaust fumes poured in through the half-open window as a red fire truck whooshed past and roared off into the city.

'We've been planning your visit for weeks,' said Charity.

'Big deal!' I said.

I hit the electric window switch and the tinted glass rose with a sigh. We drove for a few minutes in silence again. I was thinking, so it's only a visit, then. I'd be sent back to another expensive private school when the holidays were over. And why wasn't Dad here? What was he doing in San Francisco that was so important? I stared out of the window at the towering palm trees and big white houses, imagining what it would be like if I could live here with Dad all the time.

'Hey!' I said, tapping one of the giant shoulders in front. 'Put some music on!'

EXT. LYNDON AND CHARITY'S HOUSE, MALIBU — DAY. The car sweeps up the drive and stops in front of a pale, modern house that appears to be constructed of a series of stacked white boxes. CHARITY and EMBER climb out.

Dad had lots of what I call 'puddle' girlfriends (gorgeous but shallow) after Mum died, as you probably already know – it's all been well documented in the press – but he was always on tour or doing dumb stuff like flying helicopters, racing powerboats and generally being the bad boy of rock, so the girlfriends got fed up with waiting for him to grow up. They all dumped him. I don't think Dad cared too much, though. That is until he met super-perfect, clean-living, goody-goody, Charity Lane. She's definitely not a puddle. In fact, I think she has a degree from Harvard.

I suppose I didn't know what to expect. My friends at school had stepmums who were really embarrassing, always buying presents and being all huggy. Pleeease! How cringeworthy! You see, it's not like in fairy tales where the wicked stepmother locks you in the cellar. No, in the real world it's much worse than that. They torture you with attention and kindness. Aaarrgh!

'I'll show you your room,' she said, like she was the butler or something. 'You must be tired. You could sleep or have a swim if you want to.'

All the way from the airport I'd been thinking, there's something weird about her – her expression, her gestures – and not just because I'd seen her in lots of movies. She seemed to be speaking from a script, saying lines, like. . . acting.

The house wasn't what I expected either. For a start, it wasn't on Malibu beach – you know, like where all the really big film stars have houses – but up a winding road on top of a hill. It was quite modern and minimal with a kinda spiky-looking garden, a terrace and a swimming pool, in a sort of compound with a high wall around it. It felt more like an office than someone's home, because there were lots of people all running about looking busy.

My bedroom was a large, **white box** with just a bed, a bedside table, a desk and a chair. Charity opened a door opposite the window to show me a walk-in wardrobe that led to my own bathroom, another **white box**.

'We got you a computer and a cell phone. Oh, and there are some art materials over there. Your father said you'd like those. If there's anything else you need we can go shopping.'

'I hate shopping,' I said.

Charity smiled, said she had to go to 'do some work on a script', and left. I flopped down on the bed. The room was like a cell – a prison cell. There was nothing in it. Living here would be like twenty-four-hour sensory deprivation. I'd probably have to count the days by scratching notches in the wall with jagged, bleeding fingernails. I'd have to try to stop myself from going crazy by devising a reckless but brilliant escape plan. I shivered, then opened my suitcase and took out Bunny, a knitted toy that my mum made for me. I put him on the bed, changed into a swimsuit, put my jeans back on and went to explore. This holiday is going to be a complete **nightmare**, I thought.

There were four more white bedrooms with bathrooms, a study with all Dad's stuff in it, a 'screening room' with a giant movie screen, a huge open space with sofas in it (where Charity and her assistant were chattering) and a stainless steel kitchen with a cook. Yes, a cook! Strange, I thought, that Charity, a woman who doesn't eat, has a cook. I pushed at a glass door, which floated silently sideways. Out in the garden,

the sun was hot and bright and shimmering off the pool. I needed my shades, so I went back inside to get them. In the corridor, near the study, I heard Charity's voice. She was speaking on the phone.

I knew instantly she was talking to my dad.

'...trying so hard... moody... rude and miserable... come home soon, honey.'

It went quiet for a bit so I think that Dad must have been telling her something. Probably advice about how to handle the criminal stepdaughter.

'. . . OK. . . I know. . . matches. . . and knives. . .'

I crept outside again. Hilarious! They must think I'm a total psycho, I thought. Had they really hidden all the matches and knives? What a joke! What does she expect me to do, chop her into bits and set fire to her?

I strolled around the rest of the compound. Over the other side of the pool, down a path, behind some trees, was a sort of big garage. I knew Dad would have a home for all of his 'babies'. The garage doors were open and folded back. Inside was a row of gleaming sports cars and the chauffeur who drove us from the airport. He was crouching down looking at a tyre. He glanced up.

'Hey, Ember. How you doin'?'

'What's it to you?' I said. I had spotted a small car at the end of the row. 'Got the keys to the Mini?' I asked.

'Someplace safe,' he said and chuckled.

I headed back round the garage towards the terrace, and glanced through the window of a small office. On the wall was a glass box with two rows of hooks, and hanging from each hook were **car keys**.

Episode Two

Barking at Ned, Buying Orange Stuff and Not Eating Steak

INT. FUNKY, GRUNGY FURNITURE STORE, ECHO PARK — DAY. CLOSE-UP: EMBER Fury is totally fed up and gazing out of the window at the passing traffic.

Ned showed up the next day. I had assumed that maybe he wouldn't, in America, I mean, since the therapy and the drugs and all that. Ned was the only thing I hadn't talked much about in my sessions with Dr Redmond. You know when adults say they understand but they really don't; well, I knew right from the start that she just wouldn't get it.

Ned is short for Edward. He's a bit thin but still sort of cute, and has pale blond hair and blue eyes. He's the oldest of five children and he's a Londoner, like me, except he's from the East End and I'm a West End girl. I suppose you could say he's my best friend, but it's more complicated than that.

We were in this interior design store in Echo Park that was supposed to be so cool and there he was, sitting in a white leather chair, smiling at me. I hadn't seen him for weeks, or perhaps it was months, and I was so excited. I was grinning so much it made my face hurt.

'What are you doing here?' I hissed, leaning over so that I was speaking into his ear.

'I like this chair,' said Ned, stretching back and kicking his legs out in front of him. He was wearing wrinkled grey socks and the slightly too short trousers of his school uniform, although he said he hadn't actually been to school for almost a year. Over the top was the scratchy, double-breasted tweed coat that he often wore.

'Aren't you hot?' I asked. He was dressed all wrong for L.A.

'What was that, honey?' said Charity. She was carrying a cushion that was sewn all over with tiny blue and green glass beads. It was exceedingly vile. Charity was playing the over-attentive-stepmom role that day.

'Oh, I was just looking at this chair. It. . . looks comfortable,' I said, trying not to giggle. Ned was pulling a face at Charity and the vile cushion.

'So, this is what a Hollywood star looks like?' he said. 'Could do with a good meal, I reckon. She's no Vivien Leigh, is she?'

I kicked him.

'Ow! That's a nice way to greet your long lost pal,' Ned yelled, reaching down to rub his ankle.

'Who's Vivien Lee?' I asked.

'Vivien Leigh?' said Charity, thinking I was talking to her. 'She was Scarlett O'Hara, wasn't she? I love that old movie. *Gone with the Wind*. Have you seen it? The costumes are wonderful and there's a famous scene where a whole city is burning, with flames. . . Oh! She stopped and looked embarrassed. She was so lame. She couldn't even mention fires to me without blushing. Charity threw the cushion towards the chair. It hit Ned right in the face and plopped on to the floor.

'White leather?' she said, leaning down to retrieve the cushion. 'Well, if you like it, you go ahead and choose what you want for your room.'

'I hate blue,' I said, but Charity had already dashed off into the next alcove saying, 'I saw a cashmere throw over here that would be lovely.'

When I looked back at the chair again, Ned wasn't there. I spotted him over the other side of the store, next to a tall blonde woman. He was leaning on a counter, his chin resting on his hands, watching something in the woman's large red leather bag. What was he doing? As I walked over, he saw me and pointed,

'Look! A dog!'

There was a tiny, fluffy snout poking out of the bag and it began to wriggle and sniff the air. Then it opened its mouth, stuck out a tiny pink tongue, panted a bit and finally began to emit a high-pitched yapping. It was barking at Ned. That's curious, I thought.

An hour later, a team of assistants followed us out of the store carrying bags of cushions and throws and rugs, in shades of red and orange, for my new room. I quickly hid the one item I'd bought between a couple of striped lamp shades – a tin of black paint.

'Hey, Em. Did you find some cool stuff?' asked the chauffeur as he held the door open.

'Nope!' I said. 'I'd rather go to a book shop.'

'So that's what you're into, huh?' Charity asked.

'Maybe.'

'Maybe?'

'Or a gallery. More interesting than stupid shopping.'

'We could go to a museum tomorrow, if you like,' said Charity. 'Is that what you'd like to do, Em, honey?'

'Duh! Gallery, not museum,' I said, exasperated. She was so **stupid**.

INT. RESTAURANT, LOS ANGELES — DAY. CHARITY and EMBER are led to their table, meandering through the room, greeting, shaking hands with and nodding at the other, rather familiar-looking diners — actors, directors and agents.

Charity took me to lunch. The restaurant was full of plastic people. You know, boob jobs, Botox, size zeros, spray-on tans, weird pointy pixie noses – mega-celebrities mixed with desperate wannabes. The air-con was so cold it felt like you were sitting inside a room-sized fridge. All the hairs on my arms were standing up so I pulled my sleeves right down over my hands. I picked up a huge glass of water, and when the liquid hit my mouth my tongue went numb. You know when Superman blows on a river and it turns to ice? Well, that was how my throat felt when the water went down. Charity and Ned were both talking at once. It was giving me a headache. Charity was saying how she wouldn't try to be a 'mom' but was going to be my 'friend'. Huh! Just what I needed. What twisted, psycho self-help book did she get that idea from? Ned said he'd never been to a proper restaurant before. He'd only read about them in stories in comics about rich people. He was going on and on about the waiter using this electronic note pad and how he didn't understand how it worked.

'But where's the bit of paper he takes to the kitchen?'

Ned could be really dumb sometimes.

Our food orders arrived and Charity began to stir her salad leaves with her fork, then took a deep breath and asked me what I'd like to do for my birthday.

'We could fly to Vegas or drive down to Mexico or there's this fantastic spa out in the desert. . . oh, what about a little party? I know a guy who could arrange something at short notice?'

I was about to answer that I didn't care when Ned interrupted again.

'No pie'n'mash on the menu then? Ha! Don't think much of 'er plate of grass. What you got?'

'Kobe steak, rare,' I whispered. I hadn't eaten any of it as I'd only asked for it to annoy Charity, who's a vegetarian. Blood was oozing out. The plate was red with it.

'Blimey, Em! That would feed me 'ole family for a week. D'you think it's gee-gee? My mum got a bit of steak from a man down the pub. Turns out it was a horse steak!'

'Oh, shut up!' I snapped, which shocked both of them into embarrassed silence.

'Not you,' I said to Charity, and immediately regretted it.

'Ember. . . what? I haven't. . . oh, is your little imaginary friend here?' she asked and took a sip of ice water. I nodded and picked up my knife. It was too late to rewind.

'Charity, Ned, Ned, Charity,' I said, waving my knife across the table, introducing them to each other. Ned winked then stuck his tongue out at her.

'It's a good thing she can't see you doing that,' I told him.

A muscle twitched in Charity's cheek and she glanced nervously at the other diners, then slowly lifted her napkin to her mouth. It was an Oscar-winning performance.

'Shall we go?' she said.

I missed London and the Farm more than I thought I would, and I missed Daze (Daisy) and Mikko (MK) so much it actually hurt, you know, like an ache in my stomach. . . or my liver. . . or whatever organ it is right in your middle. Whether it was destiny, karma, coincidence, serendipity or fate, I don't know. . . it's one of those things where an amazing thing happens that you can't explain. Well, that was what it was, being sent to Orchard Farm at the same time as the two most incredible, extraordinary, genuine people on the whole, entire planet.

Daze always said that it was a mistake, though, her being sent there. She said it was OK to be that thin because thin people get better grades. I told her that was the stupidest thing I'd ever heard and she said no stupider than burning stuff.

Mikko was a bit like me - sent to the Farm instead of a secure unit. He'd used his mum's credit card to buy a lot of expensive and weird things online, like a gold mobile phone and the actual shoes worn by Harrison Ford in **Blade Runner**, or something. Then he'd booked plane tickets and flown to Hong Kong and Sydney and loads of other places, staying in luxury hotels and renting limousines and brilliant stuff like that. He's got that attention-deficit thingy and the psychiatrists said he's a compulsive liar and sometimes he's hyper-manic or delusional or something. Dr Redmond said he's either going to spend his life in prison or five-star luxury. That was her idea of a joke. I think Mikko is a genius and he's also a much better actor than anyone in Hollywood. No contest.

Daze ↓

Mikko ←

my page

Ember Fury. . .

alias: flamegrrl
loves: 'flame girl' comics and graffiti
hates: anything pink
my fave city: london (my hometown)
my fave food: toast
my fave movie: donnie darko

what I'm doing today. . .

listening:
firestarter – the prodigy
please, please, please let me get what I want – the smiths

reading:
the wasp factory – ian banks (on the plane)
the catcher in the rye – j d salinger

today's chat:

mk: been mixin' with the stars in LA?

flamegrrl: the stars are bogus especially the wicked stepmother from hell!

mk: what you doin' for yo[u] birthday?

flamegrrl: planning my escape

dazed: will they let you hav[e] candles on your ca[ke]

flamegrrl: ha ha ha

dazed: sorry, bad joke

flamegrrl: puppies

dazed: puppies

post r[e]

account privacy

34

The 'puppies' thing is our secret code word. The whole story is this: Mikko was making a kinda funky video for an Art Therapy project at Orchard Farm and he wanted to film someone crying over this dumb poem he'd written. But when he said 'Action' all Daze and I could do was laugh, until Mikko said we should try thinking about dead puppies. Dead puppies are probably the saddest thought you can have so it worked. The tears poured out, like non-stop, for absolutely hours and hours. Now we say 'puppies' when we mean emotional stuff like 'I miss you' or 'keep it real' or 'that was intense'.

Episode Three

Ink!, Sitting in Mud, Meeting the 'Shark' Finn and What I did to the Towels

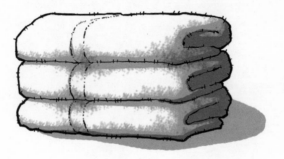

I was really bored in the house; so bored I wanted to tear my arms off just for a new experience. Charity kept suggesting places we could visit but I just said no to everything. I wasn't going to be caught in her evil web. After a while she gave up and we stayed home. Charity seemed to spend her whole day infatuated by her body. She had a trainer who came before I woke up and left at nine. Later, a nutritionist brought her lunch and, while I chewed on my daily pizza delivery, she ate a handful of bean shoots and a piece of raw fish. I guess Charity's cook must have done that catering course called 'Opening boxes and arranging stuff on a plate – 101'. Tough job!

Some afternoons she'd have a facial or a manicure or have her hair trimmed about a nanometre. She even walked on a treadmill in the evening when she was phoning the Malibu witches' coven – her obnoxious and probably equally body-obsessed friends. Tragic!

So that I didn't have to watch her emaciated carcass preening all the time, I stayed in my room, slept quite a bit and read the stack of books I'd bought at the airport. When I finished the last page of the last book, I asked Charity if I could go 'shopping' on my own. Actually, it was a big, fat lie. I needed to escape.

'OK. Take the car,' she said.

Now, before you start thinking that Charity has completely lost her mind and thrown it out with the rubbish, she didn't mean what you think. Charity was saying that I could use her *chauffeur-driven* car to go wherever I wanted. I knew that she'd probably arranged for the driver to be my minder, making sure I didn't have any fun at all, but I was desperate to get out of the wicked stepmother's clutches.

'Santa Monica, and step on it,' I said as I slid across the back seat, and the car cruised down the hill and on to the freeway. Los Angeles was sizzling hot again and a shimmering brown haze hung over the city. I'd been surfing the Net that morning and found a map of 'Cool and Crazy' places to go. 'Forget the studio tours, Rodeo Drive and Sunset Strip. . .' the website said. I was going to '. . . find the Alternative L.A.'

'Here!' I yelled. 'Pull in here!' The car drifted slowly towards the kerb and I pressed my nose against the window.

'This is it,' I said, leaping out and throwing my bag over my shoulder. 'See ya later.'

EXT. SANTA MONICA GALLERY OF MODERN ART, LOS ANGELES — DAY. EMBER Fury stands for a moment and looks up at the pale, concrete façade of the building, then pushes through the glass doors into the lobby.

The gallery was pretty cool (and I don't just mean the air-con). I wandered from room to room for a while until I found a space with a high skylight and huge, brightly coloured canvases on each wall. There were benches in the middle of the room so you could sit a mile away and kinda gaze at them, but I liked standing as close as I could, so I felt like I was inside the painting.

In a smaller room next door, a picture caught my eye as soon as I walked in. It was really tiny (the frame almost bigger than the canvas) and quite abstract – red and white dabs and scribbles. If you looked hard enough and scrunched your eyes up, you could see a sort of heart and a key shape. There was a sign beside it, low down on the wall, which said

Heart No. 1, acrylic on canvas, Amica Morton.

I jumped and let out a squeak, like
someone had pinched me. My mum!

The painting was by my mum. I wanted to reach my hand out and touch it, feel the rough surface of the paint, but there was a sort of uniformed guard bloke in the corner and he was frowning at me. He'd heard me squeak. The painting was so tiny that I started planning how I might lift it off the wall, when the guard turned away, and slide it into my bag. It would be really easy, unless there was an alarm or invisible laser beams or something. Then I saw the chauffeur standing in the doorway. Aaarrgh! I don't need constant surveillance, I thought. Why couldn't everyone just leave me alone?

I had an idea. I couldn't steal the picture but I could try something else. I stood back and looked at Mum's painting through half-closed eyes, acting like a normal person in a gallery, then strolled casually across to an archway on the other side, pretending I hadn't noticed I was being watched. Then I started to speed up, taking slightly longer and faster strides, and walked straight out the other side, skidding a bit on the polished wooden floor. I turned down a wide corridor, then round another corner, finding myself back in the lobby. I ran for the glass doors and tumbled out into the heat, then along the street. . . sprinted to the end of the building. . . sharp left. . . down an alley. I was trying to catch my breath while laughing. I'd given him the slip and I was so pleased with myself. Without my minder, I could really have some fun.

A few blocks away, I reached the Santa Monica pier and walked beside the beach for a while. It was buzzing with loads of people. I bought a can of cola from a machine outside a shop called *Venice Vibe*, which seemed only to sell stuff with 'Venice' or 'I ♥ L.A.' printed somewhere. I rolled the frosty can against my hot forehead. Venice, I wondered? The 'Cool and Crazy' website had mentioned a comic book store near Venice

Beach. I couldn't think of the address but I remembered a yellow star on the map. It had to be nearby. Just a block further and there it was, Ink!, a store that sold comics and graphic novels. I pushed open the door and went inside.

It was a lot like comic book stores in London – a mixture of Manga, Super Heroes, all the classic characters, some more trendy graphic novels and limited edition collectables in plastic envelopes. It was all so familiar. I even found a special 'UK Artists' section and my favourite character, Flame Girl.

The excitement didn't last long, though. Before I'd had the chance to have much of a look round, a menacing silver shape pulled up outside. I grabbed an issue of Flame Girl, slapped my money on the counter and snatched at the change. I was suddenly in a stinking mood. The driver looked pretty annoyed too when I shuffled out on to the sidewalk, glared at him and got in the car. He didn't say anything all the way back to the house.

Then he did something I hadn't expected. He stopped the car outside the garage but, instead of getting out to open my door, he turned round in his seat and said he'd decided not to tell Charity that I'd run away *and* that he would take me back to Ink! whenever I wanted. Cool, huh?

'Look. It's my job,' he said. 'You don't want a bodyguard, I don't wanna watch some rock star's kid all day.' He flipped his shades on to the top of his shiny shaved head. 'I was in the Marines, a cop and a stuntman. Driving you about. . . well, it's not the dumbest job I ever had but it comes close. We gotta work together on this, OK?'

'OK.'

'I'm Jerry,' he said and we shook hands.

From then on I went to Ink! every day. There was a squashy black leather sofa at the back and the owner didn't mind that I sat there for hours, reading or drawing. Sometimes Ned was there too, but he would get bored and muck about knocking over piles of books or blowing in the customer's ears so they thought he was a wasp or something. He wanted comics about football or spies and stuff, but there weren't many of those, even in the 'UK Artists' section.

The first few times I thought it was great at Ink! because I could escape and it sort of reminded me of London, but it was all wrong; too hot or too noisy or just too different. It wasn't home. I was still in Los Angeles, still miserable and still missing my friends. Only Ned made it bearable. Even though Ned was joking about all the time, being really annoying, I was glad he was there. Ned was the only thing that made me feel safe since my mum died.

It didn't take long for Charity to decide she'd made a mistake; she should never have agreed to let me out on my own. I was kinda messing up all her plans for stepmother-stepdaughter bonding, so she suddenly got all fanatical about what we could do together. She'd failed with the shopping thing (not every teenage girl just wants to shop all day, right?) and I had turned down tennis lessons and a stupid 'typhoon fundraiser' lunch. Then she tried a new angle: a weekend away.

'We're going to fly out to a spa resort in the desert tomorrow,' Charity said, flashing her perfect, neon, white teeth. 'I've invited my friend and her daughter Ruby. She's your age and I know you'll love her. We leave at six.' She paused and then added, 'But you don't have to come.'

She thought she'd ambushed me, but Charity was so transparent. First, she was trying reverse psychology, which never works. I guess she'd forgotten that I am pretty experienced in all that mind-control stuff and know immediately when someone is 'shrinking' me. Second, Jerry the minder wasn't enough humiliation. Now she was scheming to find me a 'friend' – like a dumb chaperon in one of those historical movies; the ones where women are fainting all the time because their corsets are too tight. I tried hard to think of a reason to stay in L.A. on my own, but I couldn't. I couldn't try the 'waiting for Dad to come home' angle, because he clearly wasn't. If Charity thought he'd be back soon she wouldn't be buggering off to a spa (as Dad would put it). I decided it was enough that I'd sussed her plan. I was bored, so I agreed to go. How bad could it be?

I have to admit that the resort was in a really beautiful place. It was quite swanky and exclusive and full of Hollywood stars. On the first day, I did a yoga class (which was complete torture) and floated in the pool for a while, staring at the mountains.

Here's something that will give you an idea of exactly the sort of place it was: I jumped into the pool with all my clothes on (to see what would happen) and, instead of getting yelled at, like you would in a normal hotel, Charity was handed a letter which actually apologised for not making us aware of the 'conventions of behaviour' at the spa! How weird is that? Charity showed me the letter and then gave me a brochure that explained some of the treatments we could have. They all sounded too gruesome – hot stones and seaweed wraps and thermal mud baths that sucked out impurities and scrubbed your body of toxins. Yuck!

Then Charity's friend arrived. I recognised her daughter, Ruby, straight away. She's an actress and you've probably heard of her. If you've seen a movie recently where one of the characters could have been drawn by a cartoonist – that's Ruby. She looks all pretty and sweet, like. . . well, imagine a cute, furry animal in peril, a baby deer with huge brown eyes, standing in the path of a truck – something I've often visualised since meeting her. Well, that's what Ruby looks like, but looks can be deceptive.

'Hey, Ember! I'm Ruby. I love the colour of your hair. Is it natural?'

'Yeah,' I said.

'Mine's from a salon.'

Her hair was a sort of freaky pinky-red.

'You live in London, right?' she continued. 'I was in London last year, filming. I love shopping in London. . . and Paris and Milan. I love Milan. Don't you love Milan?'

'Never been,' I lied.

I had assumed that Ruby would be a total L.A. teen horror movie and we'd definitely have nothing in common, but I guess she was trying pretty hard to be friendly, so I decided to give her a chance.

'I saw your film on the flight from London,' I said.

'Ohhh, how weird, which one?' she wailed. 'I made about four movies last year. Was it *My Werewolf High School Prom Date*?'

'No, it was, um. . . about a fashion designer, I think.' The truth was that I couldn't remember the movie at all. Just that Ruby was in it, being cute and kooky. And that it was rubbish.

'Oh, yeah! That was just the hardest shoot ever! I was, like, completely wiped out, took me for ever to recover. It was *trauma*!' She paused to take a breath. 'My mom says you were in rehab.'

I gulped. Where had she got *that* idea from? And how rude she was to just come out with it. What a cheek!

'Not rehab. Prison,' I replied, trying to keep a straight face. I'd given her a chance to be nice. Now the gloves were off.

'P-prison?' she stuttered. 'Oh. I thought. . .'

'They let me out for a holiday, but it's OK because I have this computer chip under the skin of my neck and I'm being tracked by a special prison satellite. It's really sensitive and it can tell what I'm thinking – like if I thought about stealing something or committing a murder.'

Ruby was silent for a few seconds; then she started to giggle, nervously.

'He he he, I almost believed you,' she said, not completely sure whether I was lying or not.

'No, seriously. The satellite tracks me wherever I go,' I said. 'It's scanning me right now and knows that I'm considering dive-bombing the infinity pool and splashing all those relaxing movie stars over there. It's about to send an electric shock to stop me. . .' I grabbed my throat and made a buzzing noise.

'Stop it!' Ruby yelled, laughing. 'Ember, you're so naughty!'

From then on, Ruby treated pretty much everything I said as if it was another tall tale, so when I let slip some of the real things I'd done, she didn't believe me. Probably just as well...

Ruby

On the last day, we had a manicure and I almost asked for a flame pattern on my fingernails (my friend Daze had painted flames on my nails at Orchard Farm). Then I changed my mind and chose black to reflect my mood. The manicurist had to search in the back of a drawer to find black. She said hardly anyone had black — only rock chicks — which I was quite pleased about. Ruby chose nauseating coral pink.

When we flew back to Los Angeles, Charity and her 'event organiser' began to arrange a surprise party for my birthday. It wasn't a surprise at all, of course. On our last day in the desert, Ruby and I had sat on the edge of the pool, picking the polish from our fingernails. She couldn't help herself and had told me all about what Charity was planning. I wrote in my sketchbook: Future ref. — Ruby can't be trusted.

I began to look forward to the 'surprise' party. Not for the party, which I knew would be the height of L.A. ghastliness, but because Dad would be sure to come back for it. While Charity buzzed about like a wasp with blond highlights, I passed the time ordering the weirdest take-out food I could find. I had Persian cakes that tasted of roses, fish'n'chips from the Old England Diner (not like home), all white food from the Gud Fud Deli in Malibu and pizzas with strawberries, caviar or peanut butter on them. There was a lot of complicated 'arranging on plates' for the cook to do.

Dad didn't come back.

EXT. CLUB FAHRENHEIT — NIGHT. Photographers jostle each other as guests climb out of limousines and up the red-carpeted steps into the stylish club. Broad-shouldered security men look overdressed in tuxedos. A huge, sleek vehicle glides to a halt and the rear door swings open. The noise from the paparazzi increases and the air is filled with hundreds of bright flash explosions. **EMBER Fury** and **CHARITY LANE** (and **NED**) emerge, smile and wave. . . and are guided inside.

Charity invited a load of L.A. film people I'd never met to the private lounge at Club Fahrenheit – movie stars, directors and some of their teenage offspring. I was so angry that Dad wasn't there. He was still in San Francisco. Charity promised he'd be coming later, but I didn't believe her because I knew he hadn't phoned.

The club was quite funky; all swirling red wallpaper and huge, coloured glass chandeliers. The DJ was from Manchester, which made me feel a bit better and he played some of my favourite tracks. The waiters wore long white

aprons (like they
do in those old
places in Paris)
and black bow
ties, but the
bow ties were loose, like they'd forgotten
to tie them. One of them, a bloke with
hair that flopped down over his brown
eyes, offered me a drink (non-alcoholic
– groan!) from a black tray. He smiled
and my stomach felt weird, like I was
about to burp.

That's when I saw that Ruby was there. Terrific! She came rushing over, wearing this fancy-pants dress and high heels that were way too old for her, and introduced me to her movie brat friends (that *she'd* invited to *my* party). They kinda stood in a circle, watching, like when you're at the zoo and they're about to feed the penguins or something. I could tell what they were thinking. Look at the strange English girl. Watch out! She might go crazy and burn your house down . . . or her head might explode!

Ruby was acting like we were buddies and really close, when actually she didn't know me any better than her brat friends did.

'I bet you didn't guess your mom was planning a Hollywood celeb-fest, did you?' she said, sweeping her arm outwards and tilting her head towards the throng of grisly L.A. phoneys.

'If I'd known I would have slashed my wrists or taken poison,' I said, crossing my eyes and sticking my tongue out the side of my mouth.

'You're so funny,' she said, laughing in a kinda dumb, false way.

'And she's not my mum.'

Ruby with a Mocktail

'OK, stepmom. Hey, want some tequila?' Ruby lifted her tiny sequined bag, had a quick look round (with her enormous cartoon eyes) to make sure none of the adults was watching her, then pulled out a small, squareish bottle with a yellow label. She unscrewed the top and attempted to pour some of the clear liquid into my soda. I stopped her and took the bottle from her hand, put it to my lips and took two enormous mouthfuls. Well, Ruby's friends were still staring and I had to live up to my reputation, didn't I?

Once, at school, I had a bottle of vodka in my bag for a whole term, until a teacher found it. I didn't drink much of it but I kinda carried it around, you know, for effect. Anyway, I thought the tequila would taste like vodka, but it was totally different and disgusting and burned my throat. My eyes were watering and I felt like I was going to cough and vomit at the same time. Stay cool, I thought.

'Ohhh! Ember!' said Ruby. 'You're so. . .'

'Emo?' whispered one of Ruby's friends, giggling behind her hand.

Ruby smirked and I pretended I hadn't heard and walked away.

EXT. CLUB FAHRENHEIT, FIRE ESCAPE — NIGHT. EMBER Fury exits the club through a door which is propped open. She pushes it angrily and it swings shut with a bang. There is movement in the darkness behind her, then a pop, and the glow from a match lights up a face. It's the good-looking waiter with the brown eyes. He's just lit a cigarette. He tosses the match aside and smiles.

The best thing about my party was meeting Finn, the waiter with the floppy fringe. Well, I thought it was a good thing at the time, but I guess the scary music from that shark film should have been playing, as a warning. Finn was dangerous. We met on the fire escape.

'Hey, you're Ember Fury, aren't you?' he mumbled, then took a long drag from his cigarette. Inside, he'd looked like a grown-up, but now I could see that he was probably only a few years older than me.

'Might be,' I replied, trying to be mysterious and flirty.

'Happy birthday.'

'How do you know it's my birthday?'

'Working here, remember?' he said, laughing and pointing to his apron.

'Oh, yeah, right.'

'Like your T-shirt.'

'Thanks,' I said, then giggled in a really embarrassing way, you know, with a kind of snort at the end. 'Um, it's from a shop in London,' said pig-noise girl.

A police car screamed by with its siren wailing so we stopped talking until it passed and disappeared up the street. My stomach had tied itself in a knot, like when you drink something fizzy too fast. I felt a bit wobbly and wondered

if it was because of the tequila or the boy. I reached out to grab the top of a brick wall and my fingers touched a hard, light object balanced there – a small box. I stuffed it hastily into my pocket as the waiter stepped towards me.

'Finn,' he said.

'What?' I replied.

'Finn. . . my name,' he said.

I giggled again because I was imagining a boy with fins; flipper boy, flapping about wearing a wetsuit or something. My head was spinning.

'What a dumb name,' I blurted, without thinking. He looked offended and I felt a bit bad.

'Would you like to dance?' he asked, trying really hard to smile.

'Nope,' I said. 'Music's rubbish.' When I'd walked out the DJ had started taking requests. All the adults were asking for really terrible old stuff, not even classics like Nirvana or Blur or Dad's band.

'So what music do you like?' he asked. 'I guess you're into all those London bands.'

'Actually, I prefer classical,' I lied. I don't know why, but I seemed to want to disagree with him.

'Yeah? I saw. . . *Carmen* last summer. . . which was cool, really bangin'.'

'That's opera. Opera sucks,' I spat.

'Mmm. I guess you're right.' He pushed his fringe back with his hand and laughed. 'All that singing instead of talking, it's weird, isn't it?'

I was beginning to feel quite odd, a bit unsteady.

'Would you pass the ketchup, please?' I sang in a silly, warbly, high voice, like an opera singer.

'Would you like fries with that?' he sang back.

'Large fries and a chocolate milkshake,' I sang, ending on a screeching high note.

Finn stuck his fingers in his ears and scrunched his eyes closed. 'Stop! It hurts! You'll get all the stray dogs howling!'

'Awwwooooo!' I howled. What was I thinking?

Finn pretended to run away and tried to open the door back into the club but it had slammed shut and there was no handle on the outside. At the same moment a new song started playing inside. At last, it was something I liked. I couldn't believe my luck. I was stuck outside, making a complete fool of myself with floppy-fringed opera freak, locked out of my own birthday party. Trainwreck!

Finn swore and kicked the door, then I saw the steps of the fire escape and had an idea.

'Why don't we climb down and go in through the front?'

He stabbed the cigarette into the wall and it crumbled in a shower of red sparks. He took hold of my hand and we carefully descended the metal stairs to the dark alley below.

'Don't handle the merchandise,' I said, pulling my arm away.

'I was just helping you down,' he said.

'I don't need your help, thank you very much.'

When we reached the ground, he leaned over so his face was really close. It took me a moment to realise that he was trying to kiss me.

'What do you think you're doing?' I shouted, stepping back, so that he kissed nothing but air.

'Sorry,' he said, looking embarrassed. 'Thought I'd give you a birthday kiss.'

'Well, you thought wrong,' I said.

'You sure?'

He smiled and leaned forward again but this time I was standing against the wall and couldn't escape. It was strange but, this time, I didn't want to escape. I kind of automatically tilted my head up towards him and closed my eyes. He kissed me on the mouth, his lips tasting bitter from the cigarette and making me feel dizzy. My stomach flipped over like when you're on a ride at a theme park and you're about to throw up.

'That's assault,' I whispered. 'I'll call the police.'

He stepped back, smiled and then grabbed my hand again.

'You talk funny,' he said. 'It's really sexy.'

I scowled at him and rubbed my mouth with the back of my fist. He pulled me round the corner, past the security guys and up the steps back into the club. This time I was tingling all over.

We pushed our way past all the old people on to the dance floor. Finn let go of my hand and we jumped about a bit until the end of the song, but then the track began to slow down as the DJ faded in another. This one was much slower and Finn tried to pull me towards him, but I stepped away and just let him hold my hand again. That's when his boss spotted him. This bloke wearing a serious black suit, like he was going to a funeral, came over and tapped Finn on the shoulder. I guess he must have been the caterer or something.

'Break's over. Tables need clearing,' he said angrily.

Finn nodded and went all sulky, then looked back at me. 'I'm off at eleven. Catch up with you later?'

'Yeah, OK,' I replied and he slouched off.

'What a babe!' said Ruby, appearing beside me.

'Is he? I hadn't noticed,' I lied. Her friends began to

push through the dancers and huddle round her like her fan club. They all looked at Ruby, waiting for her to speak. They were up to something, I thought. Ruby nodded at Parker, the pretty Chinese girl.

'Ember, we're all going to Battle of the Bands next week,' said Parker. 'Do you want to come?'

I thought for a moment. My head was still a little fuzzy and I was trying really hard to think of reasons to say no.

'Sure,' I said. Maybe there would be some good music. Anyway, it was another way to avoid Charity and her stupid 'I'm the perfect stepmom' routine.

'Tuesday. We'll pick you up at six, OK?' said Macy.

Finn the hot waiter →

'Hey, Rubes, what you gonna wear?' asked the very pale blonde girl.

'Designer vintage!' said Sky.

'That's so last week,' said Ruby.

'Jeans and heels!' said Parker.

They all laughed in a stupid girly way and I sighed. Airheads, I thought, and walked away.

I wandered over to sit at the bar and got my sketchbook out. I spotted Finn reflected in a mirror. He was collecting empty glasses. He waved and I grinned back like a complete idiot. I could see my face in the mirror going all pink and blotchy, then a voice in my ear made me jump.

'Who's the bloke you're goin' all soppy over?' Ned asked.

'What? Oh. . . not that it's any of your business, but he's. . . he's my new boyfriend,' I said, just to wind him up. I was a bit annoyed he'd called me soppy.

'Huh! I don't trust 'im.' Ned was lying on the bar flicking peanuts into people's drinks.

'Well, I think he's gorgeous. A total babe. Anyway, where have you been all—?'

Then the lights went out.

Ruby looks like this →

At first I thought something had gone horribly wrong, like there was a terrorist attack or something, then someone started singing. A huge birthday cake was being wheeled into the middle of the room and everyone looking at me. The cake was vile - all pink frosting and sugar butterflies, like they must have thought I was a little kid. There were loads of glittery candles and Charity made me blow them all out with everyone watching. Mega humiliation!

I made a wish. . .

. . .that they would all get out of my face.

Just after eleven, Finn came to find me, just like he said he would. He sat on a stool and leaned on the bar right beside Ned, who made a face at him.

'Hey, Red,' said Finn, and grinned.

I noticed a spot of buttercream icing on his lip. 'Hey, you've been eating my birthday cake!' I said indignantly.

'You caught me,' he said, sticking out his tongue and searching for the icing. He was about to say something when I spotted Charity out of the corner of my eye and grimaced. She was striding towards me. I leaned over on the bar, hoping she wouldn't see me. Oh no, I thought. What does she have planned now? What new evil party trick did she want me to perform?

'Em, honey,' she began. 'I think you should come and say thank you to everyone for their gifts.'

'Aw, do I have to?' I groaned.

'It would be very rude if you didn't. They've all been so generous.'

I swivelled round on my stool to speak to Finn but he was gone.

It took a million years to go from table to table saying thank you to all Charity's dull Hollywood friends. I made sure I was frowning and hiding behind my fringe the whole time. It was almost midnight when she said we should probably go home. I guess she thought it was past my bedtime, like I was a baby, or like my glass shoes were about to turn into pumpkins or something. I couldn't see Finn anywhere. Then, when I was saying goodbye to Ruby and all her phoney friends, he pushed through the crowd and grabbed my elbow.

'Call my cell,' he whispered and wrote a number on my arm with a green marker pen. Then he was gone again.

INT. ULTRA-MODERN HOUSE, MALIBU — NIGHT.
CHARITY LANE and EMBER FURY enter the vast,
white, open-plan room. Ember flops on to a
sofa. LYNDON FURY appears from the kitchen and
kisses his wife, then leans over and ruffles
Ember's hair. Grinning, she leaps up and puts
her arms round his neck.
A phone rings in another
room. An assistant enters
with the phone and hands
it to Lyndon.

'Dad, you're here!' I said.

'Did you have fun at your
party?' Dad asked taking the
phone.

'Yeah. I—'

'Just a second, babycakes,' he
said, putting it to his ear. 'Yeah?. . .
noon tomorrow. . . what a bugger!
OK. . . right. . .' He put his hand
over the phone so the person on
the line couldn't hear, then started
this whole boring discussion with
the assistant guy about going to New
York and contracts and rooms at the
Four Seasons and taking a private
jet. . . and totally **ignoring me!**
Dad talked some more to the person
on the phone then snapped it shut,
ruffled my hair again and walked
out of the room without a
backward glance.

I was so **angry**. I clenched my fists. Boiling, bubbling lava began to rise from my feet to my legs to my stomach to my chest to my chin and ears and. . . I was going to explode in a volcano of rage, burning Dad and Charity. . . and all the stupid people in the house to crispy black corpses! I had to get out. . . out. . . OUT! I pushed open the glass door on to the terrace. At that moment, if I'd jumped in to the pool, I think the resulting steam cloud when my super-heated body hit the water might have billowed out for hundreds of miles. I bet it would even have been visible from outer space. I sucked in a lungful of warm air. The house and all the spiky plants in the

garden were painted blue by the light from the pool. I pulled a towel from a pile on a lounger and stuck my face into it. It was soft and fluffy, like nuzzling my knitted rabbit. I sat down, then felt something digging into my leg and put my hand in the pocket of my jeans. I pulled out a box. The box I'd found on the fire escape. A matchbox. I pushed it open and took out a black match tipped with orange. I stroked it along the side of the box and the head fizzed and popped into life. I held the flickering flame and watched it for a moment, then placed it on top of the pile of towels. . . and went inside.

suitcase - full of
black clothes.
↓

my new
laptop↓

my idea of
interior deco↑

good
books →

When I'd
calmed down,
I texted Daze:

.ull   ✉ Messages   ▬

snggd babe @ party
EM x

Send   Options   Menu

She replied:

.ull   ✉ Messages   ▬

omg who?
D x

Reply   Options   Menu

72

Episode Four

Being Invisible, Landing Toy Planes and Walking on Crunchy Grass

INT. BEDROOM, LONDON — NIGHT. The room is dark but a thin wedge of yellow light from the half-open door is casting a narrow pool of gold on a patterned carpet. An air-raid siren can be heard wailing, up and down, in the distance.

I woke to a strange noise and the bed felt. . . different. I sat up and pulled out my earphones. The music stopped and a horrible, howling sound took over. In the gloom I could just make out the shape of the lamp beside my bed. It looked weird somehow and I was pretty certain that I'd left it switched on. Under the wailing sound I could hear raised voices, then footsteps thumping up the stairs. Ned opened the door and dashed in.

'Get up!' he yelled.

'What?' I said. 'What's that noise?'

'Air raid. Get up, Roger! We've got to get in the shelter.'

Across the room, a small child in pyjamas jumped out of the other bed and rubbed his eyes. I stood up. Suddenly, we were in thick, smothering darkness. Someone had extinguished all the lights. I put my arms out in front of me and found Ned. Ned grabbed Roger and we ran, blindly, together, down some stairs, along a narrow hallway, through a kitchen and out into a garden.

I couldn't understand why it was cold and damp outside, not warm like L.A. There were more shadows running beside us and I realised these were other children. We all moved, like a line of ducklings on a pond, along the path, down a couple of steps and through a low doorway. In the rush, I trod on someone's toe.

'Ow! That's my foot, Bill!' said a little girl.

'Sit down, Roger,' said a woman as she came through the doorway behind us. 'Right, are we all 'ere? Ned? Jane?'

'Yes, Mum,' answered Ned and Jane.

''ere, Jane. Take baby.'

I listened as the family pushed and jostled and their mother pulled a heavy blanket across the door frame. Then I heard the strike of a match and the shelter gradually filled with the soft glow of a lamp. Six anxious faces looked at each other.

WARTIME LAUGHS EVERY WEEK!

THE NEDDO COMIC

2D

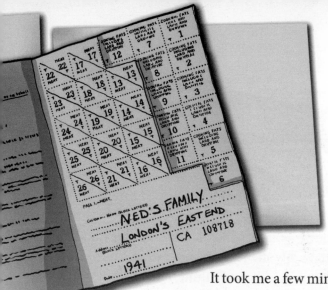

It took me a few minutes to work out who they were. It was Ned's family.

'I bet you thought this wouldn't happen, didn't you?' Ned whispered.

'Wow! We're back in London. Is this the war, with bombs and everything?'

'Of course it is. Not Malibu, is it?'

'But I don't understand. I saw a programme on telly. I thought all the children were evacuated from London.'

'Yeah. Some of the first to go. We were packed off to Dorset,' said Ned, quietly, so that the others couldn't hear. 'Me, Bill and Jane went to our cousins' farm. 'orrible it was, all mud and milking cows and diggin'. Then Mum and Roger came down too, because Mum was gonna 'ave another little 'un. But there were no bombs yet and we all really missed London, so when baby was born we came back home. Mum said if the bombs are gonna get us, they'll get all of us together.'

'Who you talking to, Ned?' said Jane. She'd heard Ned whispering. Ned laughed and I suddenly felt faint. My heart was pounding.

'Wow! Ned, I don't think they can see me!'

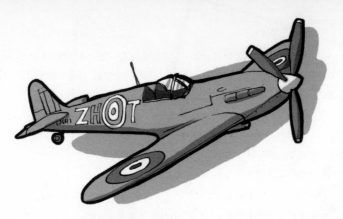

I've never known what it's like to have brothers and sisters. If you don't have any then you'll know what I mean. When I was really little it was the only thing I wished for, squeezing my eyes shut and repeating over and over, 'Please, please, let me have a baby sister.' I suppose I thought one might just turn up if I wished hard enough. The stupid thing is that, if it had worked, I would probably have hated sharing everything with some other kid, but I wished anyway.

Ned had two brothers and two sisters and they were awesome. Bill was a mischievous ten year old, who told disgusting stories about pilots with no heads and blood gushing from the stumps of severed limbs. Ned kept telling him to shut up because he was scaring little Roger, but I don't think Roger was listening. Roger was five and adorable. He carried a sort of metal box which was full of model planes. He knew all their names and the sounds that they made. He flew them round our heads, diving down to skim the puddle of muddy water on the floor and roaring up again to land on a runway on the fold of a blanket. The quiet one was Jane. She had her face close to the pages of her book, which had an elephant on the cover. When Bill pretended that his guts were falling out and nudged Jane's elbow, she just sighed and swatted at him with her hand, as if he was an annoying fly.

'Grow up, Bill,' she said, glancing up at the roof like a grown-up, in a way that made her seem much older than eight. Kitty, or Kitten (really Katherine), was the baby.

'What's that noise?' I asked Ned. I could hear footsteps outside, heavy boots or something, because I could feel the thump of each step.

'It sounds like the docks again,' he said.

'The docks?' I said, 'No, there's someone outside.'

'Surrey Commercial. Getting closer now.'

'What do you mean?' I asked. 'What's getting closer?' The thumping was getting louder and little Roger was frozen with his hand in the air, listening. He had a plane clutched in his fist and I realised, with a growing feeling of terror, that the sound wasn't feet but bombs exploding; bombs dropped from planes.

'There'll be incendiaries, Mum. I should be out there,' said Ned. His face was pale and sick-looking and he was scratching at his hand in a nervous way.

'You stay where you are,' said Mum, touching his hand to make him stop scratching. 'There'll be plenty of time for that after the all clear.'

There was another thump and the shelter shook.

'Closer,' said Bill. 'Hope they get the school.'

'Bill, that's a horrible things to say,' said Mum.

'But I don't wanna go to school any more. Ned doesn't, so why should I?'

'Ned's doing his bit at the fire station,' said Mum.

'I'd enlist if they'd have me,' said Ned.

'Yeah, me too,' said little Roger. 'RAF. Spitfires. Yeeeooowww!'

He flew the plane past my face. The shelter shuddered again as the next bomb impacted nearer than the last. Roger jumped on to the bed beside Ned and pulled the 'runway' blanket up around his ears. Everything rattled.

'That was close,' said Mum as she stopped the lamp from toppling over. Then the stamping feet moved away again.

'Is it over?' I asked.

'Over?' Ned replied, scratching his hand again. 'It's just started.'

The pounding went on for hours, punctuated by another sound, the anti-aircraft guns just a few streets away. It was terrifying – like the sound of someone's music turned up really loud coming through the wall, or something – but this music was deadly. How could they go through this night after night, I thought? Roger and Jane managed to get some sleep. Mum made some tea on a little stove and she, Ned and Bill played a card game called gin rummy. I couldn't work out the rules. It was very early in the morning when we heard the wailing noise again. This time it was a single, sustained sound, that didn't rise and fall.

'All clear,' said Mum. 'Ned, will you carry Roger? I'll take baby.' She pulled back the heavy grey blanket and looked out into the soft sunlight that was filling the garden. We headed back to the house. Halfway up the path, Roger woke up and squirmed out of Ned's grasp.

'I want to check Thumper,' he said, trotting towards a sort of wooden box on legs by the back gate. Bill followed him and pulled open a door in the front of the hutch and reached inside. He showed us the grey-brown furry occupant. It was an enormous rabbit. Ned and I stood on the lawn yawning for a bit and looked up at the house. There was a dusty taste in the air and the grass seemed crunchy, like there was sand sprinkled on it.

'It was Nelson Street got it,' said Jane, running breathless from the kitchen. 'All our windows are gone in the front. Mum says it's a good thing we left the doors open or the blast could have been worse.'

Ned was watching Bill as he handed the rabbit back to the smallest brother. Bill walked towards us up the path, grinned at Ned and drew his finger across his throat.

'Stop it!' said Ned.

'Stop what?' said a voice from the kitchen. A tall man wearing a khaki uniform appeared in the doorway.

'Dad!'

The man laughed and crouched down to give Jane a hug.

Their dad had been given weekend leave from his army regiment and had been on his way home the night before when the air-raid siren sounded. He'd left Paddington station and set off to walk home, but had to take cover and spend the night in a packed public shelter in the City, sitting on the stairs.

'Got to be back Monday morning,' he said. 'Can't tell you where we're goin' but couldn't face months of lookin' at the ugly mug of our sergeant major without huggin' me nippers and kissing the missus first. Right, Mum?'

'Right,' said Mum, leaning over to pick up his bag.

The baby, who was still sleeping, was placed gently in a basket in the kitchen and Dad, Bill and Roger set about clearing up the glass in the front parlour. Mum and Jane collected the ration books that they needed to get food and headed off to the butcher. Ned stood in the hall, fidgeting. He was all jittery and worried-looking.

'Go on,' said Dad. 'Get on over to the fire station. I bet they could do with some extra help today. I'll be here when you get back.'

'Righto,' Ned shouted, and he dragged me out of the front door and down the street.

Episode Five

Floating Buckets,
Fighting the Sea Creature's Tentacles
and the Pie

There was rubble everywhere. The pavement crunched with glass and dust. Several houses had broken windows like Ned's but, oddly, some were completely undamaged. At the end of the street we turned into a narrow lane and went downhill. We could see clouds of brown dust and black smoke up ahead. The smell was terrible, sort of sweet and bitter at the same time.

'They got the warehouse,' said Ned. 'That's burning sugar you can smell.'

The fire was the biggest I'd ever seen. It was a huge brick warehouse next to the Thames. Through the smoke I could just make out two boats on the river, which were spitting jets of water up at the walls, but there was no sign of fire engines on land. A line of people were handing buckets of water to each other trying to douse the flames in a wooden hut beside the dock. Inside the hut, I could see the blackened skeletons of an armchair and an old-fashioned hat stand, a hat still hooked on it, wrapped in flames. The people were doing what they could with their tiny line of buckets, but it looked futile.

'Ned!' yelled an old man at the end of the line. 'Get over to your fire brigade mates an' tell 'em they're needed here. They're in Nelson Street.'

'Righto, Mr Richards,' Ned replied, starting to jog back up the lane. I followed. We ran for what felt like miles, but it was only a few streets – it was just so hard to run because of the bricks and roof tiles in the road. Nelson Street was in chaos. We heard it long before we got there. A whole row of houses and shops was ablaze. People were shouting and the sound of the fire was deafening.

There were three fire trucks in the road and a team of men wearing tin hats running about connecting hoses. Ned ran to one of them and tugged his arm. I couldn't hear them above the din but watched as the man pulled his arm free and shouted something at Ned. The flames were mesmerising. It was like a sort of sea creature with tentacles curling around the window frames and chimney stacks. It was totally awesome, like special effects in a disaster movie.

Ned ran back and pulled me away, the way we'd come. I wanted to stay and watch the dancing flames but Ned looked really anxious, so we started jogging back towards the docks.

'They can't spare an engine. Too many fires. Half the engines are two streets over where it's even worse. See, I told Mum last night, didn't I? I knew I'd be needed. Incendiaries,' he said, out of breath.

'What're incendiaries?' I asked.

'Fire bombs. Some of 'em have timers so they go off after the firemen get there.'

'That's terrible,' I said, horrified.

'That's Hitler,' he said.

We arrived back at the dock with the bad news about no spare engines and Ned joined the line of buckets. I soon discovered that I couldn't help. If I'd picked up a bucket it would have appeared to float in space and would probably have freaked everyone out. It was quite a shock, being invisible. I'm like a ghost, I thought.

It was well into the afternoon before the exhausted group had managed to save the hut and damp down some of the surrounding buildings. The warehouse continued to burn, but more fire boats had arrived and the blaze wasn't as fierce as before. The burnt sugar smell still coated our throats.

'There's not much more we can do here,' said Mr Richards. 'You go on home, Ned, and help your mum.'

'My dad's home,' said Ned proudly.

'All the more reason, then.'

All the neighbours were out in the street when we got back. Dad and Bill had been helping to put boards and blankets over the broken windows. Women and children were busy clearing up the damage, some using coal shovels, spades and brooms to sweep dust and broken glass into metal buckets. Mum, Kitten in her arms, was talking to the woman from next door.

'It must be lovely having hubby home,' said the neighbour.

'Just wish we could have had a nice Sunday dinner for 'im,' said Mum. 'He's off again on Monday and who knows when he'll be home again.'

'I've got a tin of corned beef you could 'ave.'

'No thanks, Lil. You keep it. We've got plenty of veg from the garden.'

'Nothing at the butcher's then, Mum?' asked Ned, walking up the path.

'He'd just sold the last chops and sausages,' said Mum.

Ned went over to his dad. They both held their fists up and did some pretend boxing, then Ned leaned over and whispered in his dad's ear. Dad nodded and they went into the house.

As the sun went down, you could still see the red glow of the burning warehouse above the rooftops. After a supper of thick slices of bread and cups of tea, the children went straight upstairs to bed. All of us were in the back bedroom now as the front had no windows. We fell asleep with the reassuring murmur of Mum and Dad talking downstairs.

It was bliss when I woke the next morning to find I was still there. I know it sounds strange, but I was much happier in bombed-out London than I had been in Malibu, surrounded by swimming pools, chauffeurs and designer clothes. There hadn't been an air raid overnight and everyone was bubbling with the excitement of having the whole family together for Sunday dinner.

By noon, potatoes had been dug up from the garden, scrubbed and put on to boil. Carrots had been collected from a crate under the stairs, cleaned and chopped, and there was a pie in the oven that smelled delicious. Ned and Jane set the table.

'We don't have enough forks,' said Jane.

'Yes we do,' said Ned. 'Six.'

'What about your friend?' said Jane, smiling. 'The one you've been talking to all day.'

Ned laughed and chased her round the table. Mum was just getting the pie out of the oven.

'That's enough of that!' she said, holding the steaming dish over her head. 'Call everyone; we're ready to eat.'

Jane ran to the front parlour where Dad, Bill and Roger were playing snakes and ladders. Dad was sprawled in a big brown armchair, laughing. He'd just gone down another snake.

'Pie's ready,' said Jane, and they all followed the mouth-watering cooking smells into the kitchen.

The pie was delicious. Well, it must have been, because although I didn't eat any I saw that everyone else had shiny, clean plates. Dad mopped up the last of the gravy with a slice of bread and Roger picked up his plate and licked it when his mum wasn't looking. They all had these stupid smiles on their faces and the loud chattering there'd

been all morning had become a chorus of sighs and happy giggles. I had fallen in love for the second time that week, fallen in love with the whole family. And that's when the terrible thing happened.

It was just a tiny gesture. Bill turned to Ned, pointed to his plate and wrinkled his nose. . . like a rabbit! Ned tried to hide a laugh behind his shirt collar, then he pulled a stupid face at Bill and licked his lips in an exaggerated way.

'Mmmm,' he said.

'Shhh,' hissed Mum indicating the younger children with her eyes.

I felt sick. I knew what the tiny gesture meant, but I couldn't believe it. It was so. . . repulsive!

'Thumper!' I yelled. 'You've eaten Thumper!'

Episode Six

A Limousine, Loads of Lip Gloss
and the Lead Singer's Identity

EXT. POOLSIDE, MALIBU HOUSE — EARLY EVENING.
One of the loungers is missing and there is a
large black stain on the terrace in its place.
EMBER FURY sits on the remaining lounger, under
a parasol by the pool, wearing jeans, sneakers,
a striped jumper, and shades. She is engrossed
in a book and miserable. CHARITY LANE exits
the house and joins EMBER under the parasol.

'I know you're upset about your dad not being here, Em,
but this moody act is. . . well. . . it's just a bit. . . childish,
isn't it?'

I said nothing and hunched over my book. She
was wrong. I wasn't upset about Dad any more. I was
feeling completely traumatised by Ned and his evil,
rabbit-eating family. I couldn't get the picture out
of my head, of Bill wrinkling his nose and Roger. . .
licking his plate! It was like a cannibal horror movie or
something. THEY ATE THE RABBIT!

'I'm not angry about the fire,' said Charity, folding her
arms and looking angry. 'I just don't understand. . .'

There was a long pause.

'Ruby called. . . She says she's left you lots of messages. I
thought she'd be a nice friend for you, while you're in L.A.'

While I'm here, I thought. So that meant I wasn't staying.
They really were going to send me back to another school,
or back to Orchard Farm and the therapy sessions. I rolled
over on the lounger, away from my wicked stepmother. My
stomach rumbled really loudly. I was starving hungry because
I hadn't eaten anything since returning from London. At
Orchard Farm, Daisy told me that she once lasted for more
than a week, only drinking water and eating slices of apple. It
hadn't been quite that long since my disgusting birthday cake.

96

Flashbacks of the rabbit pie made me feel sick, but I didn't think I could refuse food for much longer.

'I wish you'd eat something,' said Charity, like she was telepathic or something. 'How about some fruit?'

I shook my head. I wasn't going to surrender. Charity sighed and went back inside. She'd given up and I'd sort of won, but it didn't feel much like a victory.

I closed the book. It was pretty hard to read in the blazing afternoon heat with sweat running down my back. As well as not eating, I had also refused to change out of my jeans and sweater. I'd been wearing them for almost three days, because I knew Charity hated them and because I loathed all the other clothes in my wardrobe – clothes that she had bought. I reached under the seat for my MP3 player and was about to listen to some music, when the wicked stepmother came out again.

'Em, do you know anything about a limo that's at the gate for you? They say you're going to a concert.'

'Ruby!' I exclaimed, remembering the invitation.

'Ruby?'

'Yeah. You happy now?' I said rudely. 'She invited me to this thing called Battle of the

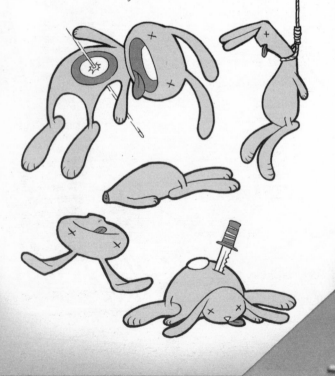

Bands. I forgot.' I stood up. At least I could get away from the house for a few hours. I went to my room and opened the walk-in wardrobe. It was now full to bursting with clothes and shoes. Charity probably thought she could buy my friendship, or something. Not a chance!

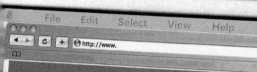

my page

Ember Fury. . .

alias: flamegrrl
loves: a waiter called finn (I think)
hates: ned the rabbit-murderer!
my fave city: london (my hometown)
my fave food: don't mention food!!
my fave movie: donnie darko

what I'm doing today. . .

listening:
nirvana
the killers

reading:
the melancholic death of oyster boy – tim burton
flame girl in hollywood – raven blaze

today's chat:

dazed: the babe @ your party, did he call you yet?

flamegrrl: no don't know what to say if he does?

dazed: you haven't told me anything about him like who is he? an actor?

flamegrrl: actually, he's a waiter

dazed: be careful! don't meet him on your own and go somewhere you know and definitely don't go to a hotel!

post reply

I looked at myself in the mirror. I had unwashed, greasy hair and a massive oozy yellow spot on the side of my nose, but I wasn't going to give up my protest. I wouldn't wear any of those stupid clothes. I swore, slammed the wardrobe door and picked up my bag. I stuffed my mobile and sketchbook inside and headed for the limo. The enormous black car was parked by the house, having been let in through the gates, and the chauffeur opened the door for me to climb in. It seemed to be full of girls wearing identical expensive outfits – denim, coloured leather jackets and lip gloss. I wondered for a moment if I'd made a huge mistake.

'Em!' yelled Ruby as I found a space next to the pretty Chinese girl. 'You remember Parker. . . and Macy. . . and Cate. . . and Sky?'

'Yeah. Hi,' I said, feeling completely stupid that I hadn't at least changed my top and brushed my teeth. Thank goodness the limo was air-conditioned, so I wasn't sweating so much any more. We glided out of the driveway and headed down the hill. The girls were chattering about a teacher at their school who was going to be a judge at the Battle of the Bands.

'He actually brushed my arm!' said Sky. 'It was an accident and everything, you know, he got really embarrassed, but it was *soooo. . . sensual*!'

'He's got such a pile of junk car, though. How can you like someone who drives a pile of junk?' said Ruby.

'It's retro,' said Parker. 'A VW Rabbit. It's retro.'

'No, it's a pile of junk. Anyway, why would he be interested in you,' said Ruby, with a sneer.

'I heard he was in a boy band,' said Macy.

'No, it was a TV show *about* a boy band,' said Cate. 'Or was it that soap he was in. . . I dunno.'

'I don't care. He touched my arm!' said Sky. They all groaned.

I looked out of the window. We were pulling up beside a kind of sports arena, a giant gymnasium. There were yellow and red banners hanging everywhere, saying *Battle of the Bands*.

'We're here,' said Cate, reaching for the door.

'Wait, let the chauffeur open it, dummy,' said Ruby. 'What's the point of arriving in a limo if you're not going to do it properly?'

'Sorry,' said Cate and sat down again.

So we did it properly and sailed into the building, the crowds of teenagers standing outside parting in front of us. Ruby and her entourage got a load of these 'wow, look who's arrived' looks. I felt like a nerdy, spotty, greasy freak beside them but actually it was quite nice not to be the centre of attention.

INT. ARENA, 'BATTLE OF THE BANDS' — EVENING. The arena is packed with noisy teenagers. There are very few adults. EMBER, RUBY, MACY, SKY, PARKER and CATE walk in together. There are steep banks of benches on both sides and a stage in the middle. The girls climb up the steps. A man with spiky hair is on the stage, tapping a microphone.

'Are you gonna be like staying in L.A.?' asked Macy.

'I hope not,' I replied.

'Oh. Because, well, you know, I was gonna say, you should come to our high school. It's like the best high school in L.A.'

'Hello. . . is this on? Hello, everyone. I'm DJ Del from OVFM Radio.'

The whole place shouted back at the man with spiky hair, like a load of brainless idiots.

'Welcome to Ocean View's Battle of the Bands, sponsored by OVFM Radio and Candy Kiss Cosmetics.'

They roared again.

'There are eight bands competing tonight.'

Screams and whistles.

'Before we begin, let me introduce you to the panel of judges. On the left, it's Mr Rosenberg, the performing arts teacher at Ocean View High School.'

The beam from a spotlight whooshed across the stage to the people sitting at a long table below us. The teacher, Mr Rosenberg, held up his hand, more to shield his eyes than to acknowledge the cheers.

'That's him!' said Sky, grabbing my hand. 'That's the teacher who touched my arm.'

'Well, he looks a real dork in that sweater,' said Macy.

'Shut up!' said Sky, pushing Macy out of her seat. 'That's the man I love!'

'Ms Lauren Kiss, from Candy Kiss Cosmetics. Jake Strong from Target Records, who will be offering a recording contract to our winners.'

More cheers and whoops.

'So, let's get the party started. Put your hands together for the Surfers.'

Four blond kids climbed on to the stage and plugged in their guitars. They all looked like they'd just come from a day on the beach or at a skate park and from the first chord I could tell they would be terrible. Each band was going to do a ten-minute set, playing three or four songs. Halfway through the Surfers' first song I wished I hadn't come. I was thinking of ways to sneak out and call Jerry the driver to come and pick me up. Then they started playing some old song from a hundred years ago, 'Surfin' USA', which they played loud and thrash-metal-style and everyone rose to their feet, singing along. I stayed seated. Two more songs later, as the crowd cheered and whistled, the Surfers' left the stage and I left the arena. Outside, in the lobby, was a stand selling drinks. I bought some water, and when I twisted the top it fizzed up all over my sweater. The second band was starting their set inside. They sounded even worse than the first. I found a bench, sat down and rummaged in my bag for my mobile. I scrolled down and found Jerry's number but then changed my mind. I didn't want to go back to the house yet. They all hated me. Charity hated me because I was rude to her and I was the moody teenage stepdaughter who had set fire to her garden furniture. Dad must hate me too because he didn't seem to want to hang around in the same city as me, let alone the same house. And now I'd fallen out with Ned, too. It made me shiver, thinking about Ned. How could they? How could they have killed and eaten their pet? It was barbaric. And Ned thought it was all a big joke. I hated him!

My phone beeped. Just when I thought I couldn't feel any worse, I had a text from Mikko.

I replied,

I jabbed my thumb on the send button and had begun to look in my bag for my sketchbook or something to read when the third band started.

They sounded good. Sort of punky, a bit rocky, and the singer was brilliant. I ran back inside. This was more like it. I pushed my way through the crowd.

Everyone was going wild. I strained to see what the band looked like. It was four guys with messy, floppy hair, wearing skinny jeans, black leather and striped jumpers. They looked awesome. According to the red letters painted on their drum kit they were called the **Next Big Thing**. Corny, I thought, but kinda cool.

'Em,' yelled Ruby. 'Do you see who it is, the singer?'

'No, I can't see,' I said.

'It's that waiter. The one from your party.' She said it in a weird way, as if she knew I really liked him. Maybe she'd seen me dancing with him.

'Finn?' I asked. 'Do you mean Finn?'

I stood on tiptoe and leaned forward. It *was* him. Wow! It was Finn who had that amazing voice and was up there looking so cool. My heart was drumming against my ribs and the flipping-stomach feeling came back, just like when I met him on the fire escape. He reached the end of the first song and leapt into the air. The crowd

yelled and whistled so much you almost couldn't hear the last
deafening chord.

'Big Thing! Big Thing! Big Thing!' the audience began to
chant.

'I'm in love,' said Parker, clutching her chest.

'I saw him first,' said Macy.

I was furious. He's mine, I thought. He was the only cool person I'd met so far in L.A. He was different. He was funny and unpredictable and exciting and maybe even dangerous and he kissed me in the alley at my party. I was the one who was in love with him. I still had his phone number written on my arm like a fading bruise. The next song started with 'one, two, three, four' from the drummer and then the thump of a thunderous beat. We all jumped up and down and the floor shook. The rumble of feet hitting the floor was like the bombers flying overhead in London. The sound was terrifying and exciting at the same time. I was sweating again but I didn't care about having a shiny, spotty, red face. This was the most fun I'd ever had in my entire life!

The song came to a crashing end and Finn threw off his T-shirt. It landed in the crowd and the girls at the front screamed. But DJ Del grabbed the shirt, climbed on to the stage and angrily told Finn to put it back on.

'Awww,' moaned the girls.

'I wrote this last one for a babe I know,' said Finn, brushing his wet fringe out of his eyes. A steady drumbeat started, then a rolling bass line, joined by a guitar riff that was quite sad, melancholic. . . and sensational! Then Finn started singing with a sort of fake London accent. He sounded really dumb, but it made me feel sick with excitement. He'd written it for a 'babe' he knew and he was singing it with an English accent! OMG!

My girl is cool and fa-a-amous,
She hates the paparazzi,
Her nose is kinda se-e-exy,
Think about her all the time.

I'm really not a stalker,
I haven't got a shrine,
OK, it's just a small one.
Red, you're mine, you're mine!

Big Thing's guitarist

Cra-a-azy about you,
Ma-a-ad about you,
Tell my shrink about you.
Crazy about you,
Mad about you,
Crazy about you.'

Did he say Red, you're mine? Red? He'd called me
Red at my party. Was the song about me? I felt like
I was drifting; above the crowd, towards the stage, into
his arms. As the song ended, I was screaming too. The
applause went on and on.

'Give it up for the Next Big Thing,' said DJ Del.
Then he started waving his arms up and down, trying to
calm the crowd. 'I guess you quite liked them.'

The screaming erupted again. Three microphone stands
were being placed at the front of the stage while Finn's
band were unplugging their instruments.

'OK. These three girls are from
Pacific Palisades. . . Booty!'

Big Thing's drummer

Three gorgeous black girls strutted on to the stage and took up positions draped over each other. Then a funky backing track started up. The girls bounced in the air and started a brilliant dance routine. They were amazing and when they started singing they sounded great too.

I couldn't watch. All I could think about was Finn. He had left the stage and disappeared into the dark, but he was in the building somewhere. If I could find him, maybe he would be pleased to see me. He might talk to me, even try to kiss me again. I found my phone and rolled up my sleeve, but it was too dark to see the numbers on my arm. Was that a five or an eight? Why hadn't I put it straight into my phone after the party? Because I'd set fire to towels and spent two days in the middle of World War II,
that's why!

'Calling a cab?' said a voice behind me.

'I can't. Someone is blocking the light,' I shouted at the irritating person standing in the way. I looked up. It was Finn.

'I saw you in the crowd,' he said, grinning.

'You. . . you were. . . great. . . a-a-amazing,' I spluttered, feeling like a total idiot. I had forgotten all about trying to act cool, but I did remember the horrible spot on my nose, so I held my hand over it.

'Won't win,' he said, glancing at the girls finishing their slick routine.

'Why not? Everyone loved you,' I said, through my hand. I was being really gushy and creepy. It was tragic!

'The competition,' he said, hooking his thumbs in the belt loops of his jeans. 'Fixed. Well, not fixed exactly, but they already have a manager. They'll get the contract.'

'That's completely bogus,' I said. 'So unfair.' I tried to calm down.

'Hey, Finn,' said Ruby as she and her giggling gang surrounded him.

'Hey, girls, whassup?' he said with a really cool flick of his fringe.

'We thought you were totally fa-a-antastic,' said Sky, trying to copy Finn's fake London accent from the last song. My song. They all laughed.

'I've gotta go,' he said. He smiled at Ruby, then took my hand and dragged me through the crowd and down the steps.

'Do you want to kinda, you know, meet up sometime?' he asked.

My heart was beating really fast again.

'You mean, like a date?' I said.

'Well, yeah. Like a date. . . only more confusing,' he said, mimicking me with his fake London accent. My face began to feel as hot as sunburn, but I still wanted to give him an enormous hug, even though he was making fun of me.

'So what makes you think I want to go out with you?' I said, pretending I wasn't interested.

'Oh, well, I. . . I don't know. I just thought you might like me to show you some of the sights of L.A.'

'I've seen them.' I kinda wished I hadn't said that as soon as the words came out of my mouth, but then I had an idea. 'How about tomorrow? Can you meet me tomorrow morning, ten o'clock?' I asked. 'Do you know a comic book store in Venice. . . Venice Beach, called Ink!?'

Episode Seven

Driving to Las Vegas, a Mustard Kiss
and the Red Rock Monoliths

EXT. INK! COMIC BOOK STORE, VENICE — MORNING.
FINN is waiting on the sidewalk. He's looking for
a chauffeur-driven limo. A flash of red catches
his eye. Nestling between a sleek Mercedes and
a brooding Lexus is a red dot, a Mini with a
target painted on the roof. Finn watches as it
nips ahead of the other cars and swerves in to
the kerb. A tinted window glides down.

'Get in,' I said, grinning at him.

I knew that he would be waiting for a completely different car. He thought I'd have a chauffeur or arrive in a taxi, so his reaction to the Mini was perfect. His mouth was wide open in amazement. It was hilarious.

'What are you doing?' he said, sounding worried. 'You're too young to drive.'

'It's extraordinary the skills you can pick up at a posh English boarding school these days,' I said, in my best classy accent. 'Don't just stand there. Get in!'

He opened the door and got in beside me, still looking really anxious.

'We're going to have an adventure,' I said. I pressed my left foot down on the clutch, moved the gear stick into first and gently pushed the throttle down a bit. The engine growled and I slowly raised my left foot. We pulled smoothly away from the kerb and I pressed down harder on the throttle. The Mini roared up the street.

'I thought we'd be meeting for a soda, you know. . . maybe talk about what music we like, our favourite comic book characters. . . or something,' said Finn, nervously.

'Flame Girl,' I said.

'What?'

'Flame Girl. My favourite comic book character.'

There was silence. I suppose he was trying to decide whether the weird English girl was going to be cute and fun or a total psycho.

'Come on then, Flame Girl,' he said, laughing at last. 'Where d'ya wanna go?'

I found out pretty quickly that I didn't have any idea where I was going. When I'd decided to steal the car (which was frighteningly easy, by the way, in a house that's completely full of security cameras and bodyguards), I had to think of somewhere we could meet that I knew how to get to. It had to be Ink! because it was the only place in L.A. I'd been driven to more than once. But now I was completely lost. Finn was still laughing at me, which was better than when he'd looked worried, but I wanted this date to be romantic, not a joke.

'Well, if you want a real adventure, I guess we have to get out of the city. Go right here,' said Finn, pointing to a ramp that led up on to the freeway. There was a lot of traffic but I managed to merge into the slow-moving line of cars heading north.

'What's your dad going to do when he finds out you took his car?' Finn asked.

'How do you know it's his car?' I said.

'Well, you didn't hot-wire it in the street, did ya?'

We were both silent for a while. I was concentrating on the road.

'Will he call the cops?' asked Finn.

'Dad's not in L.A. I suppose someone might. Call the police, I mean. I guess Jerry's gonna notice that the car's missing eventually,' I said. 'But I don't care. Let's get as far away from them as we can.'

Finn didn't look convinced at all. Just at that moment, the traffic seemed to clear and the road opened up in front of us. We decided to head for Las Vegas. Las Vegas sounded glamorous and a bit dangerous. We could definitely have an adventure there. Finn switched on the radio and pressed a few buttons, and the CD changer whirred somewhere in the back of the car. At least I knew Dad would have some cool music. We were just passing a sign that said *Las Vegas 200 miles* when I saw something flicker in the rear-view mirror. It was Ned sitting in the back seat. He smiled and raised his hand in a sort of wave.

'Hi, Ned,' I whispered. Although I was still angry about the rabbit pie, I'd really missed him. I was glad he was back.

Here's what we listened to the most:

```
disc 01 track 04:  blur - song 2
disc 02 track 02:  supergrass - caught by the fuzz
disc 05 track 01:  lou reed - perfect day
           track 02:  talking heads - road to nowhere
disc 06 track 09:  garbage - stupid girl
```

It was all pretty old stuff but classic and great for driving. The second track on disc 02 seemed to be Finn's favourite, which might have been a sort of premonition.

'Let's stop,' said Finn.

'What?' I said.

'Let's stop up ahead at that diner. I'm real thirsty. Look, there. Pull in at the diner.'

We'd been travelling for a while, an hour or maybe more, through the hills and then on to the desert highway. There was a low building ahead of us and lots of signs beside the road saying *Aunt Mitzy's Famous Diner* and *Best Burgers in California*. I swung the car off the road and parked beside a white truck. I was quite glad to stop because I'd just driven further and longer than I'd ever done before, on the wrong side of the road, and the concentration had been *killing*.

Inside we sat in a kinda booth with sticky red plastic seats. Finn picked up the menu. A waitress in a pink gingham dress came over.

'I like your car,' she said. 'Aren't you a little young to drive?'

She must have seen me get out of the driver's side, I thought.

'I'm twenty-three. I look young for my age,' I said.

'Can I get a cheeseburger, fries and a Coke?' said Finn.

'Aren't you going to sing it?' I asked, reminding him of our first meeting on the fire escape. He looked up at me from under his fringe and the corners of his mouth turned up in a gorgeous, wonky smile.

'Can I just have some water? No ice,' I said.

The waitress frowned at me. 'You sure have a cute accent. You British?'

'Yeah.'

She walked away and I found myself wondering why she hadn't taken Ned's order and then I laughed at my mistake.

'What's funny,' Finn asked.

'Nothing. I might tell you when I get to know you better.'

When Finn's burger arrived I looked at my glass of water and felt really hungry, like my stomach was this huge, empty, echoing room with a bit of dust on the floor, so I ordered some pancakes. Finn didn't say much while we ate and Ned was silent too. It seemed like they were both trying to decide what to say to me. I liked watching Finn eat. His hair hung down over his eyes and all I could see was his mouth moving around, chewing at his burger, like a lion with a big chunk of zebra. A bit of ketchup and mustard escaped and his tongue darted out and left a slick of spit on his lip. I imagined him leaning over and kissing me again. This time his kiss would be mustard flavour. Mmmmm.

Finn sat back and pushed his plate away. He was looking out of the window and he suddenly put his hand into his pocket and pulled out a wallet. A couple of pieces of paper and a photograph fell out. He found the folded bills he'd been looking for and slapped the money on the table. Then he gathered up the bits that had fallen out. I glanced at the photograph, which was of a girl, and I thought it looked a bit like Ruby.

'C'mon, let's go,' he said, already out of the booth. He was pointing out of the window at a police car that had pulled up near the Mini. There were two cops and one of them was standing by our car, looking inside. I slid out of the booth and swung my bag on to my shoulder. On the way past the counter, I waved goodbye to the waitress.

'They may already be looking for us,' said Finn as he pushed me through the door.

'Don't be ridiculous,' I said. 'We've only been gone a couple of hours.'

'Bye, hon. Give my love to Prince William,' called the waitress.

'Morning, officer,' said Finn, taking the keys from me and getting into the driver's seat. The cop nodded.

'Your vehicle?' he asked.

'Yeah. Graduation present,' said Finn.

'Drive safely, now,' said the cop, grinning at us.

Finn turned the key in the ignition, then looked down at the gear stick and the three pedals. He didn't know how to drive a car that wasn't automatic.

'Are they still watching us?'

The cops had gone into the diner. They were standing at the counter talking to the waitress but looking out of the

window at us. Finn was stirring the gear stick around and the engine was making a horrible grinding noise.

'Push the clutch down,' I said. 'Reverse is over to the right and back. Gently lift your foot.'

The car pulled backwards and spun round with a jerk, then Finn found first gear and we lurched on to the highway. Once we were out of sight of the diner I put my hand on the wheel.

'Pull over!' I yelled. 'We can't drive all the way to Las Vegas in first gear.'

Ned was laughing so much in the back seat that he was doubled over and clutching his stomach.

I took over the driving again and gradually the buildings thinned out and disappeared until empty desert stretched out in front of us – mile after mile of red sand. I wanted to stay on the main routes but Finn was paranoid about the cops back at the diner, so eventually I turned off the highway. I pushed my foot down on the accelerator to go faster. I wanted to drive as far away from Malibu as I could.

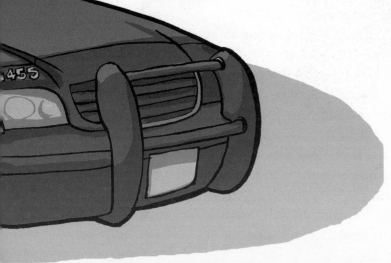

We were approaching another small town. It was *very* small, just a crossroads really. Finn had his head down, searching for a radio station, when I saw the sign; *Pepper's Hardware*. I had stopped the car and was halfway across the sidewalk before he looked up and noticed I was gone. He sprang out of the car and got to me just as I was pushing at the door.

'Hey, what are you doing?'

'We'll need some provisions if we're gonna have an adventure,' I said.

'Provisions? Like what?'

'I dunno. Let's see what they've got.'

I wriggled out of his grasp, leaned on the door and walked into the gloom.

I thought it was going to be a bit like a DIY store back home, with gardening stuff and bathroom tiles and pots of paint, but the first thing I spotted was an axe.

'You planning to chop down some trees?' Finn asked, arriving beside me.

'Maybe.'

Further along was a little camping stove. Next to that, on another shelf, were a rolled-up tent and a folding canvas chair.

'I thought we were heading for Vegas,' said Finn. 'You won't need a tent in Vegas.'

'I suppose not,' I said, and strolled over to the next shelf.

There was a noise at the back of the shop and a door opened. A man with grey hair and a moustache walked in carrying a stack of boxes. He put them on the long counter that stretched across the full width of the store.

'Hey there, folks! What can I do for you today?' he asked.

'Um. . . we're just browsing,' I said, which is what I always say in shops when I want to be left alone. Actually, I'd seen exactly what I wanted, but I took a while to decide what colour to get. My choice finally made, I stacked all my items on the counter.

'I'll take these, thanks.'

Finn had been gazing into a glass cabinet in the corner (I couldn't quite tell, but I think it was full of guns), and he turned round and asked me, 'You got money?'

'No, but I've got this,' I said, taking Charity's credit card out of my bag.

With two strides, Finn was beside me again, holding my arm.

'Where'd you get that?' he whispered, sounding angry. 'Did you steal it?'

'No!' I said. 'Well, actually yes. But she won't mind.'

'Em, you're trouble!' He reached into his pocket and pulled his wallet out again. He counted out enough to cover my purchases and steered me back to the Mini. I thought he was going to get really furious with me, but he seemed to just stop and change his mind. On the road again, he went right back to being nice, as if he'd never even seen the stolen credit card.

He relaxed a bit and we started talking, although I guess I did most of it because he was doing that thing that boys do sometimes, y'know, answering a question with as few words as possible.

'You're a waiter then?' I said.

'Summer job.'

With some effort, I found out that he'd taken the job to meet people in the music business. Working for a caterer was the best way to network in L.A. because record company bosses and film executives had so many lavish parties all the time.

'Are you still at high school?' I asked.

'Yup.'

Next year he wanted to go to college, UCLA or film school or something. I told him I wanted to go to college, too, art college in London, but I wasn't sure if Dad would let me. I asked about his band and how they got together.

'What I really want is to record my own songs,' said Finn, using more words than he'd uttered for the last hour.

'You should come and meet my dad,' I said.

'Yeah?'

Finn became quite excited, talking about Dad like he was his greatest fan. He had all Slap!'s albums and posters on his bedroom walls and everything. I made a face because I thought he was being a bit sad and geeky. I took my eyes off the road for a moment and watched him as he adjusted his shades and raked his hand through his hair. Then I pressed my foot down and we began to go faster again. We ploughed along the road, which had become more of a dirt track, throwing up clouds of dust behind us. The breeze lifted Finn's

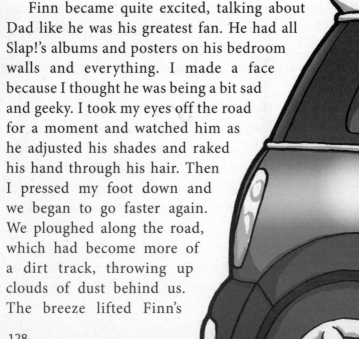

fringe and a muscle twitched in his cheek. He was soooo gorgeous! I felt dizzy and kinda nauseous. This is love, I thought. I'm in love!

I started to wonder about what being Finn's girlfriend was going to be like. He hadn't actually said it, but that was what I was, wasn't I? If he'd had a girlfriend already, why was he running away with me to Las Vegas? I thought about the picture in his wallet. She was an ex. . . or his sister or cousin or something.

'**Stop!** Stop the car,' yelled Ned from the back seat.

I slammed on the brakes and we skidded to a halt. The Mini was surrounded by a swirling yellow cloud and it took a while to clear.

'Ember! Why did you do that?' Finn exclaimed, rubbing his forehead. He'd had his feet up on the shelf and folded forward, held by the seat belt, crashing his temple against his knee when I braked. I turned round and looked at Ned.

'Why did you shout?' I asked.

'Look,' said Ned.

He pointed out of the car at the clearing dust. Gradually the windscreen was filled with the most amazing landscape. We were on a track that edged a deep canyon snaking to the horizon. Carved monoliths of red rock, like resting giants, lay across the desert. The sky was an intense, deep blue and everything glowed in the low, late afternoon sunshine. It was amazing. We got out and walked to the edge then stood in silence for ages, just looking at the changing colours.

'The sun sets in the west, doesn't it?' said Ned.

'I think so,' I replied.

'You've been driving the wrong way, then,' he said.

'Are you sure?' I asked.

'Sure of what?' said Finn.

'Ned thinks we're lost,' I said.

'Ned?' said Finn.

'You know that thing I was going to tell you when I knew you better?'

'I don't understand.'

'Ned. Ned's the thing I was going to tell you about. Ned's a friend of mine. He sort of visits me sometimes. But, well, no one else can see him.'

Finn didn't say anything. I felt like my heart had dropped down into my shoes. I held my breath. I was such an idiot. It was too soon to have told him. How could he ever love a crazy, orange-haired freak now that he knew she had an invisible

The light had changed. Finn released me. The sun was setting and the sky was filled with an orange glow as if the edge of the earth was on fire. Ned and Finn stood either side of me and, at the exact same moment, they both reached out and held my hands!

'Wow!' said Finn.

'Double wow!' said Ned.

I sighed. 'Puppies.'

133

Episode Eight

The Psychopath with an Axe, the Missing Walls and Explosive Consequences

EXT. 'KOOL MOTEL', DESERT — NIGHT. Headlights pick out spiky aloe plants and the almost human shapes of tall cacti as the Mini draws up at a modest adobe building. It has a wide veranda.

I don't know how we found the motel. When we eventually climbed into the Mini it was almost dark and Ned thought we should try to go back to the highway. But, even with the headlights on, I wasn't sure if we were on the right road or even on a road at all. Just as I was thinking that we'd probably be lost out there for ever (and found, months later, three desiccated skeletons sitting under a cactus), we saw the sign. It said *Kool Motel*.

'Shall we?' Finn asked.

'What, get a room?' I said, mortified as soon as I said it. I hadn't really thought about the consequences of running away with Finn. If we got a motel room, maybe there would only be one bed. FLASHING DANGER SIGN! It was exactly what Daze had told me not to do. I started wondering about

how you might feel if you were sitting in an aeroplane, about to do a parachute jump. You'd be thinking that you wanted to do it, to see if hurtling towards the ground is really as great as everyone says, but that waiting to step out into the air is kinda the most terrifying experience you've ever had. . . and maybe you need more training.

I drove up close to the veranda. Apart from the hotel sign there were no lights on anywhere.

'There's no one here,' said Ned.

'Do you think it's closed?' I asked.

'Why would they put the sign on?' said Finn.

'Maybe it was switched on by a psychopath trying to lure unsuspecting tourists to their **bloody deaths**!' I suggested.

'That's not funny,' said Finn.

We got out and tried the door of the first cabin. It was locked but Finn took two steps back, jumped forward and kicked at the centre of the door, just like a stunt man in a movie. It swung open and he went in.

'Have you found the psycho with the axe yet?' I called.

'Cut it out!' he replied, obviously not amused.

137

'Wait,' I said and ran back to the car. I'd had an idea. I opened the boot and felt about in the dark. I came back with a large black torch, the type you can prop up at the side of the road when you have a flat tyre or something.

Inside wasn't what I expected at all. I waved the beam of the torch around looking for Finn, but the circle of light revealed nothing – an empty room. Finn had disappeared!

I nearly dropped the torch and it sort of flipped up so that the light pointed in the air. There was no roof, only the dark desert sky and a few dim stars. Then Finn appeared and made me jump half out of my skin. There was no back wall either. He was standing in the desert.

'Aaarrgh! You scared me,' I said.

'Looks abandoned,' he said.

'A film set,' I suggested, which I thought was a pretty brilliant deduction, because I'd remembered that sometimes they build a whole town for a movie, but it's only the fronts of the buildings, not proper rooms or anything.

Finn said that it was no good trying to get back to L.A. and we should stay there until the morning, then disappeared again.

'I don't trust him,' said Ned.

'Don't be stupid. He's the coolest and gorgeousest person I've ever met,' I whispered back. It must have been quite a loud whisper though because Finn said 'What now?' from somewhere outside.

'There's no such word as gorgeousest,' said Ned. 'He wants something. . . and I don't mean you-know-what.'

'Shut up! It's none of your business, anyway. I don't need your permission.'

Finn strolled back into the roofless, backless room carrying a white plastic garden chair. He was mumbling something under his breath. He threw the chair down and stamped into the dark again. His mood had changed. He was like a different person.

'What's he so angry about?' I asked.

'Maybe he's hungry?' Ned suggested.

'Oh, well that's OK,' I said, reaching into my bag. 'Look, I've got chocolate and chewing gum.' I tipped out some of the other things we'd bought at Pepper's. There was a bar of chocolate, a bottle of bright orange soda, a double pack of chewing gum and a green camouflage print sun visor.

'Not exactly a banquet,' said Ned.

Finn arrived back with a second chair, put it down several metres away from the other one, and sat in it.

'Here,' I said. 'D'you want some chocolate?'

Finn groaned, then mumbled, 'I could be at home eating my mom's steak right now. Instead, I'm stuck in the desert with a weirdo who talks to herself.'

'All you had to say was no thanks.'

I couldn't work out what I'd done to annoy him. He sat in silence, staring into the darkness. All the things I'd been so certain about, just hours before, seemed to be crumbling away.

He should have been looking after me, saying he'd keep me safe in the dark, all the things a boyfriend is meant to do. Maybe he wasn't my boyfriend after all. Perhaps there *was* someone else in L.A.

'When we get back, will you invite me over?' he asked.

That was better. He wanted to come to the house. It was OK. I relaxed a bit and asked, 'Are we going back, then?'

'Course we are!' He sounded quite irritated again.

'But I thought we were running away. . .'

'No, we're not.'

'We could go to New York. . . or to London instead.'

'Don't be an idiot, Em,' he said with a horrible half-sneer, half-laugh.

'But we haven't even got to Las Vegas yet,' I said miserably, sounding like a spoilt little child who didn't get the present she wanted.

'We're not going to Las Vegas.'

'Yes we are. We just have to find the road again. . .'

'We can't, Em. Gotta get back. I've got a job tomorrow in Beverly Hills and a date w—'

'**What**?' I felt a cold hand run down my back.

'No. . . forget that,' said Finn, realising that he'd said the wrong thing. I wanted to sink into the ground and never come up for air. I had just worked it all out. I knew now why he'd asked me out. It was as if I'd known all the time and the horrible truth had been lurking there in a dark corner in my head and a curtain had been drawn back to reveal a hideous, drooling

fiend. He'd added the final piece of the puzzle and the whole monstrous scheme leapt out. All the stuff he'd told me about his band and needing to make connections to get a recording deal and coming to the house – it made perfect sense now. I remembered the photograph in his wallet – the picture of someone who looked like Ruby. It *was* Ruby. I hadn't wanted to believe it but I knew now it was true. I'd been so stupid. . . so deluded.

'You only made friends with me to meet my dad, didn't you?' I whispered.

He didn't answer, just cleared his throat.

'And Ruby is your girlfriend, isn't she?'

'Mmm. . . yeah,' he said. 'Sorry, Em. I know it was. . . kinda cruel, but it seemed like a good idea.'

'Yeah, right. Flirt with the stupid English girl with the famous dad, pretend you like her. . .' The cold feeling was being replaced by a boiling, steaming rage. I threw the torch across the fake room. It missed Finn and crashed against the wall.

'Hey, watch it!' he yelled. 'Ruby warned me you were a headcase.'

I looked around for something else to throw
and picked up the bottle of soda.
It caught him
on the shoulder
as he pelted for the door.
Then I followed
and began to chuck
the entire contents
of my bag at him.
He stumbled
along the veranda,
holding his arms up
to deflect
the flying phone,
a curled-up paperback,
a pot of cherry lip balm,
my sketchbook,
a plastic dinosaur
and my MP3 player.

'Crazy Brit kid…
you need locking up,'
he said, sort of laughing.
'That song…'
I shouted.
'It was for Ruby
wasn't it?'
There was only
one object left,
my final purchase
from Pepper's
Hardware,
clutched so tightly
in my fist it left
dents in my palm.
I opened my hand.
A box
of matches.

Episode Nine

Finn's Five Minutes of Fame
and the Massive Fight

So here we are, back on page one. You know the rest of the story: the fire, the rabbit, crashing the car, getting a face full of airbag, the cops showing up and arresting us, my ripped-out heart. Just turn back to the beginning if you've forgotten.

My memory of that night, in the police station in the desert, is really fuzzy and mixed up. I think I had to answer a lot of questions from all sorts of different people, but I was tired and confused and I don't remember much of what I said. Finn and I were separated, then my dad showed up and things got kinda serious. I couldn't help it, but I started giggling to myself because I had just realised that my adventure with Finn had started on a fire escape and ended *escaping a fire*. Yeah, I know it's not that funny, but you have to understand that by then I was getting a little bit hysterical. The cops were explaining something about following us from the diner to the hardware store and losing us in the dark. I tried to listen but the voices became muffled and then I was floating over the room, looking down at the top of my head, on the dust on a filing cabinet in the corner and on the empty coffee cups on the desk.

Then suddenly I slammed
back down into my body and jerked awake,
like a patient being given an electric shock. Everything was in
focus again, clear and crisp.

What?

What did he say? Who should be dead? *We* should be dead?
If I hadn't seen the rabbit and turned the wheel at that moment
and we hadn't crashed the car in that spot, we would have
plunged to our deaths over the edge into the canyon!

Flamegirl
escapes again

RIP

Select   View   Help

account   privacy   logout

my page

Ember Fury. . .

alias: flamegrrl
loves: true friends
hates: finn the fake
my fave city: london (my hometown)
my fave food: chocolate cereal
my fave movie: donnie darko

what I'm doing today. . .

listening:
portishead
cocteau twins

reading:
the gossip mags – all lies

today's chat:

mk: where are you?
            what's happening?

dazed: are you ok? are the rumours
            true? please reply we are
            worried about you

post reply

Dad was silent all the way back to Los Angeles and I pretended to be asleep. When we finally reached the house, Jerry had to drive the car slowly through a crowd of photographers and TV cameras by the gate. Someone had leaked to the press that I'd taken Dad's car and run away. I couldn't believe it at first, but we found out later, of course, that it had been Finn on his mobile. As soon as it was established that he was neither a car thief nor a kidnapper, Finn had come straight back to L.A. and done all these interviews with every news channel and gossip magazine and become the most famous person in town. . . for about five minutes. I was a bit of a celebrity for a while too. You probably read the stories. They were mostly fiction, you know, so I guess you understand why I had to put the record straight.

Well, now you've heard my version – the truth! Finn got a manager and a record deal, so I suppose, in the end, he must have thought that ripping my heart out had been worth it. Did you like his first single? I did. I'm glad he didn't record 'Ruby's Song'. I don't think I could have coped with that.

Dad was furious about what I'd done and everyone in the house seemed to be glaring at me all the time. I got sick of the attention so I kinda crawled into bed and slept for about a hundred and fifty years. When I woke up I heard Dad and Charity having this loud argument. It was awful.

'You know, don't you, that if she wasn't your daughter she'd be in jail by now. . . or worse! You don't see how she's manipulating you. . . .'

She started yelling that we'd been really lucky. I thought she meant about not driving into the canyon, but it was something about the movie company's being about to destroy the 'Horror Motel' film set in the desert so it had been easy to pay them off. She said Dad wouldn't be able to just throw money at every disaster I caused.

I *knew* it, I thought. I guessed right. It *was* a fake motel for a movie. I was stupidly feeling rather pleased with myself when I heard Charity say, 'I'm leaving.' Then she stormed out of the house, shouting that Dad needed to get me some 'help'. As she got in the car, Dad said,' I know,' in this really quiet voice.

That was the first time I cried. Not because of what she'd said, but because Dad wasn't defending me any more. He knew it was all true and so did I. A few minutes later I heard a knock on my door.

'Em, are you awake?'

'Go away!' I said.

I suppose I could have ended this book here but what

PART 2 SURVIVAL KIT.
CHECK LIST

☑ WATERPROOF MASCARA
☑ SAFETY HELMET
☑ CARBS - CHOCOLATE AND BISCUITS
☑ MOBILE (HELPLINES ON SPEED DIAL)
☑ HI-FACTOR PROTECTION - 'SAD' BLOCK
☐ FLEECE BLANKET
☐ FLUFFY SOX

happened next, the second part of my story, is even more extraordinary, although this time the best bit didn't make the news. In fact, you're the first person I'm going to tell, so prepare yourself.

Episode Ten

**White Stripes, No Bruises
and Balloons on Dog Leads**

INT. NED'S KITCHEN, LONDON — DAY. It's a sunny summer afternoon. The back door is open and a light breeze is lifting the pages of the newspaper on the table. NED and EMBER sit opposite each other. The house is silent. No one else is home.

When I found myself in London again, it was no comfort at all. I was just glad that I wasn't in Los Angeles any more, with all the bad stuff that was going on there. I was sitting beside Ned at the kitchen table, the same place I'd been last time, when I'd watched them eating that gruesome pie. This time we were alone and Ned was leaning over something black and dirty lying on a sheet of newspaper. He seemed to be fixing what looked like a thick, oily necklace.

'What's that?' I asked.

'Come on. I'll show you,' he said, grabbing the object and heading for the hallway. I followed him out of the front door and into the sunshine. Resting on its side in the front garden was a large black bicycle. Ned wrapped the necklace, which I now saw was a bicycle chain, over a cog and fiddled with something in the middle of the back wheel.

'They got it for me at the fire station. Said if I fixed it I could ride between the crews and the ARP with messages. I might even get a uniform,' he said proudly.

'A mobile phone would be much easier,' I said.

He turned the pedal round a couple of times and then stood up, lifting the bike at the same time.

'There! Let's go up West,' he said, grinning.

I stood over the front wheel then climbed up to sit on the handlebars with Ned's arms either side of me, and when we were balanced we set off along the street, heading for the City. I knew what he meant by 'up West'. He meant that we were going to the other side of London, my side of London, the part I knew, where I grew up.

First we went along the road beside the docks, where the sugar had been burning in the warehouse fire. How long ago had that been? A week, months, a year? It all looked completely different. More buildings had been damaged so there must have been lots of air raids and bombs since the last time I was there.

We passed St Paul's Cathedral and I leaned back so I could look up at the dome. Round the corner Ned skidded to a halt just in time to avoid a bus coming the other way.

'You idiot!' yelled the bus driver, leaning out of the cab.

'That was a close one,' said Ned.

I'd fallen off and was sitting on the road, a bit dazed.

'I think it hit me,' I said. 'But I'm not hurt.'

I'd felt the bus knock my shoulder

and throw me on to the ground but there was no bruise, and no mark on my elbow where I'd fallen against the kerb. I brushed the dust off my jeans and got back on the bike.

There were lots of people everywhere, going in and out of the shops, and cars and buses whizzing by. It was sort of familiar but not quite the same. Lots of people were wearing uniforms but they all seemed happy, not miserable or serious like they were worrying about the war. Some office buildings had walls of sandbags outside, and the edge of the pavement and some of the lamp posts were painted with white stripes. There were posters everywhere, but these didn't advertise trainers or fashion brands or mobile phones. They said things like *Careless Talk Costs Lives* and:

Suddenly, I recognised something.

'I know where we are!' I yelled.

It was odd somehow. We were definitely in a part of London that I knew. I'd been there before.

'There!' I yelled. 'That's the comic book shop!'

It wasn't, of course. The building that I recognised, where Graphic Planet should be, had brown crosses of tape

all over the window and seemed to be selling suitcases and umbrellas.

The sun was hot and Ned was tired so we got off the bike and began to walk.

'Ned? Why did you kill Thumper?' I asked.

'I didn't. Dad did it.'

'You know what I mean,' I said. 'Your mum made a pie out of that poor rabbit.'

'That's what it was for,' said Ned. 'To eat. It's just the same as the meat you get from your soupy-markets. We just grew it in our garden, that's all.'

'But I thought it was Roger's pet.'

'Yeah, Mum didn't have the heart to stop him playing with it. But she said it would make it really hard when they had to wring its neck, after the little ones had fed it and looked after it and everything.'

'Did Jane and Roger know what they were eating?' I asked.

'No. We told 'em Thumper had run away. Dad left the hutch door open so it looked like he'd escaped. You don't know what it's like with rationing. We don't have meat that often and when we do it's 'orrible. We're all sick of bread and potatoes every day. I can't just go into a booger bar when I want something to eat, like you.'

'Burger not booger, you dummy,' I said, laughing.

'Anyway, it was really tasty. Best pie we'd had in ages.'

'OK, I get it, you were hungry,' I said, but actually I was thinking what's the problem living without meat? Vegetarians do OK, don't they?

'It was quite funny, watching you turn green,' said Ned.

'Still, it wouldn't matter how hungry I was. I would never, ever eat a rabbit,' I said, folding my arms.

'Not even a little tiny paw?' said Ned, holding up his little finger and wagging it in my face.

'Stop it!' I said.

'Not a teeny, tiny bit of fluffy tail?' he said, wiggling his bottom.

'Ned, don't! You're a sick weirdo,' I said, pushing him off the pavement. He almost lost hold of the bike and had to swerve round a man wearing a long coat and a brown hat.

'Watch out!' said the man.

Ned pulled a face, then grinned and did a sort of dance along the kerb.

'Come on, let's go and see the balloons.'

We went across the river.

'My friend Daisy lives in that mansion block over there, with her mum and dad. . . and sister,' I said. 'Their flat looks out over that park.'

'Not yet, she doesn't,' said Ned.

'Oh, no. I suppose not. Not for another sixty years.'

We cycled on, under the railway bridges, then up the hill towards Clapham Common.

159

'There they are,' said Ned. 'The balloons.'

'Where?' I asked. I was looking for a fun fair or a kid's party. I couldn't work out what Ned was talking about. 'What balloons?'

'Barrage balloons. There,' he said, pointing in the air, up ahead.

Snaking across the sky above the common was a river of giant silver spaceships; obese shapes that rippled and glimmered in the afternoon sunshine. As we got close, we could see that they were tethered on long dark cables, giant dog leads stopping them from escaping. It was like a sort of balloon 'fat camp'.

'Wow! They're amazing,' I said.

'They're supposed to keep the bombers away, but Mr Richards reckons they can do more damage than bombs when they break free. They'll knock your chimney down or even take the whole roof off, given a bit of a gale.'

There were lots of other things on the common that Ned wanted to show me. He pointed out the searchlights, like chunky torches the size of a van, that made a light so bright it could sweep across the sky looking for enemy planes. They were just like the ones you get outside a Hollywood movie premiere, I thought.

'Over there're the ack-ack guns,' said Ned, pointing at some distant shapes. 'Those huts are where the crew live and that there is the ammunition bunker.'

He'd obviously been there lots of times before. Why do boys get excited about that sort of thing? I kinda stopped listening and daydreamed a bit about the time that my mum brought me to a circus in a big tent on the common. It was the type that just has amazing acrobats with ropes and trampolines and flying cars and all that.

Episode Eleven

The House-sized Crater, the Balancing Wardrobe and Ned's Bread and Butter

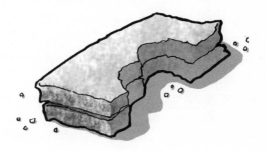

We didn't hear the explosion. The first thing we heard were the bells on the fire engines, far in the distance. For Ned, it was like Pavlov's dogs – you know, the scientist guy who made dogs drool by ringing a bell. The dogs thought they were going to get fed, or something. I don't remember exactly. Anyway, Ned froze on the spot and began scratching at his hand like he'd done that night in the shelter. He got on the bike and started to look round, searching the horizon. A cloud of black smoke was beginning to fill the sky, back the way we'd come.

'Looks like a big one,' he said as I climbed back on to my perch. The fire was a couple of miles away but we could hear it long before we got close. There were lots of people running about; an ARP warden in his black uniform, firemen carrying rolled-up hoses, a woman pushing a big blue pram, even a shopkeeper wearing a long apron. Some were running away from the terrible noise but others were going towards it, like us. I could feel the ground shaking as we came round the corner just as a wall collapsed about a hundred metres away. An ARP warden stood in the road with his hand raised to stop us. We couldn't go any further. It was too dangerous. We were south of the river, not in Ned's patch, so he didn't know any of the fire crews. We had to just stand there in the street, watching the inferno.

CITY OF LONDON POLICE

DANGER

UNEXPLODED
BOMB

EXT. STREET OF TERRACED HOUSES, LONDON — DAY. It appears as if the whole world is on fire. In the middle of the terrace, like a gap in a row of teeth, there is a house-sized crater, where a house should have been. All the buildings in the row on either side are empty shells and every house or shop is ablaze. There are numerous fire engines, hoses and firemen filling the street, tackling the blaze. Their task seems impossible.

'Must have been a UXB. We haven't had a raid for days,' Ned shouted over the deafening sound of another wall tumbling down.

'What's a you-ex-bee?' I yelled.

'Unexploded bomb.'

The firemen were crouching in pairs or dangling from the tall ladders, grappling with snaking hoses, directing powerful water jets into the flames. They were so close I was terrified the next whoosh of fire would engulf them. The blaze was spreading, out of control, and houses opposite, across the street, drenched in a rain of falling sparks, were beginning to burn too. A large group of people had gathered around us, all watching in horror. I wondered if some of them were looking at their own homes burning. We were all pushed back further down the street and I could tell Ned was frustrated that he couldn't do anything. He was getting really agitated and nervous.

'Let's go round to the other side,' he said, and I followed him back through the crowd and down an alley. We found a fence that had been crushed by a fallen chimney and passed through into a row of small back yards. It was quieter but we could still hear the shouts and roar of the fire, and feel the heat through the walls.

'What's that?' I said.

Ned stopped and looked at me. 'What?'

'I heard a child crying,' I said.

I tried to work out where it was coming from. There was no one about back there, behind the houses, and the faint sound seemed to echo round the walls.

'Over there,' I said, pointing at the house across the next yard. The noise was coming from upstairs.

As we got closer, we heard a rumble and a crash. Ned dropped the bike, climbed over a pile of wood and ran into the building.

'**Wait, Ned,**' I called. '**What if it's not safe?**'

Inside there was a staircase spiralling up to a hole in the roof where you could see the blue sky above. Ned was already halfway up and calling out to whoever was up there. He disappeared through a doorway at the top. There was black smoke pouring out and up through the hole. When I reached the top step and went through into the room I could see the streets below and the rows of burning buildings opposite. The whole front wall of the house was missing and there were fallen roof beams and piles of bricks everywhere. A wardrobe was leaning out, balanced on the edge with a red dress still attached to the handle, fluttering on a coat hanger. A bed with blankets flapping was hanging in mid-air, half the floor gone beneath it. The air was filled with dust and choking smoke. I couldn't see Ned, just a little girl who was hopping about and crying.

There was a hole in the wall to the right, where the smoke was coming from and I could hear the crackle of the fire. A chest of drawers had fallen over and was almost blocking the hole. **I dashed towards it but was thrown back by a sudden curl of flame that spat out at me like a tongue.**

'They're stuck!' the girl was yelling. 'Get them out! Get them out!'

'Ned, get out of there!' I shouted. 'The building's going to collapse.'

169

I pulled the girl back towards the stairs. There was a crack and a black figure appeared and climbed over the chest of drawers, out of the fire. It was a small boy, coughing into his sleeve, his face tucked into his elbow.

'John,' said the jumping girl. 'Where's Georgie?'

'The fireman's gone to get him,' said John, coughing again and wiping his eyes.

They were talking about Ned. The children thought he was a fireman. There was another crack and the building shook.

'Ned! Please, come out,' I screamed. I could feel the heat of the flames burning my skin. The children could feel it too and began to crawl backwards towards the stairwell. There was a rumble and the floor began to move. The bed and wardrobe toppled and disappeared over the edge. The walls were falling, a deadly cascade of bricks. 'Ned!' I cried as a blanket of smoke wrapped itself around me.

EXT. WIDE, TREE-LINED, SUBURBAN STREET, LONDON — DAY. A pretty semi-detached house has been badly damaged by fire. The burned-out shell is still smouldering. An old woman and a young girl are sitting on a couple of green kitchen chairs which have been brought outside. There is an ambulance in the street and two men wearing white coats, wellington boots and tin hats emerge from the house carrying a stretcher.

I don't remember how I got to the burned-out house. I was in a different street in another part of the city. I suppose I could have walked, but I don't remember doing it and I soon wished I hadn't. It was awful. The roof and windows of the house were gone and the green paint on the front door had bubbled like blisters and peeled off. I felt sorry for the little girl and the old lady. Then I felt even worse when they brought the body out on a stretcher. The wind blew the blanket back a bit and a curl of blond hair escaped. It was the same colour as the little girl's and I think it must have been her mum. Her mum was being carried into an ambulance, just like mine had been. Oh, no!

Please don't be dead, I thought.
Please wake up,
please wake up!
I felt dizzy and my feet seemed
to loose contact
with the ground.
I began to float…
float upwards.

EXT. GARDEN OF NED'S HOUSE, LONDON — DAY. ROGER is sitting quietly on a pile of sandbags outside the half-buried, turf-covered Anderson shelter. BILL comes through the back gate and stops to sit beside his younger brother. ROGER moves over to give him room. EMBER stands on the lawn looking up at the house. She appears confused. She walks up the path and into the kitchen.

Jane was laying the table in the kitchen. She smoothed the cloth and put the knives and forks down carefully.

'Go and get Bill and Roger,' said Mum, putting the bread board and a small loaf in the centre of the table. Jane walked out of the back door into the garden.

I was back in Ned's kitchen and a bit puzzled, wondering how I'd got there. Nothing felt real any more.

'Are you all right?' asked Ned. He was standing by the window.

Ned was OK. I was so relieved. I thought he'd been crushed inside the building.

'How did we get back here?' I asked.

'I'm not sure,' said Ned, looking rather perplexed.

Roger and Jane came in from the garden. They weren't mucking about or laughing as usual.

'Sit down,' said Mum. 'There's jam today, from Mrs Gale. I couldn't say no.'

Bill came up the garden path holding a small flat parcel wrapped in white paper. He sat down next to his sister and handed the parcel to Mum.

'Ham from Mr Evans,' he said quietly. 'Because our brother's a hero.'

Ned was looking at the knives and forks on the table but he wasn't sitting down. Then Jane got up and went

over to the cutlery drawer in the dresser. She picked out a knife and fork and came back to the table where she put them neatly in Ned's place.

'Thanks,' said Ned with a sort of nervous laugh. 'I thought you'd forgotten me.'

He sat down.

'Jane, what are you doing?' said Mum.

'Setting a place for Ned,' said Jane.

Mum's eyes filled with tears.

'This is strange,' said Ned quietly. 'I think I'm dead.'

'What?' I said.

'I'm dead. They can't see me.' He was waving his hand in front of Bill's face.

'I don't understand. I can still see you, so how can you be dead?' I said. I was starting to feel sick.

'I died. . . in that building,' he said, getting suddenly to his feet.

'You can't be dead,' I shouted, trying to grab hold of him.

Ned was ignoring me, dancing about and sticking his tongue out at Roger and Mum. They weren't reacting. Ned spun round and then stopped and stood still, looking at something on the kitchen dresser. A newspaper.

'Look,' he said, almost inaudibly.

I went over and looked where he was pointing. The newspaper was folded so that only two columns on the front page were visible.

The small headline at the bottom read:

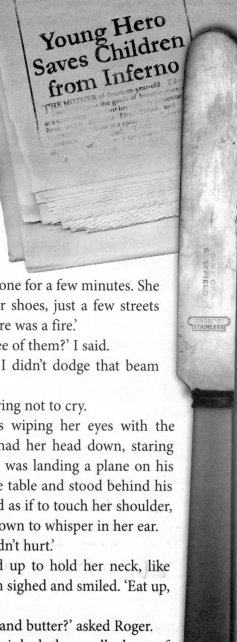

Young Hero Saves Children from Inferno

THE MOTHER of fourteen-year-old Ed...

'At least I got them all out,' he said quietly, leaning over to read the article.

'What happened?' I asked.

'I'm not sure. I think the children were trapped when their roof came down. Their mum had left them alone for a few minutes. She was standing in a queue for shoes, just a few streets away, didn't even realise there was a fire.'

'You saved them, all three of them?' I said.

'Yeah. But it looks like I didn't dodge that beam after all,' Ned chuckled.

'It's not funny,' I said, trying not to cry.

At the table, Mum was wiping her eyes with the corner of her apron. Jane had her head down, staring at her slice of bread. Roger was landing a plane on his slice. Ned walked round the table and stood behind his mother. He put out his hand as if to touch her shoulder, then hesitated and leaned down to whisper in her ear.

'It's all right, Mum. It didn't hurt.'

Mum brought her hand up to hold her neck, like she'd just felt a draught, then sighed and smiled. 'Eat up, Roger,' she said.

'Can I have Ned's bread and butter?' asked Roger.

Ned looked at me and winked, then walked out of the kitchen, down the hallway and through the front

door into the street. I followed him, my brain spinning, bewildered. I had a lump in my throat and my chest hurt. I could hardly see and my eyes were itching with tears. Ned stood in the middle of the road and looked up at the sky.

'I think I'm gonna go then,' he said.

'What do you mean?' I asked.

'I'm off, movin' on.'

'No! Don't leave me,' I sobbed. I was starting to understand what he meant.

'It's all right. I'll be around, Em, keepin' an eye on you. Hey, I'll be there any time you feel like setting fire to something.'

I laughed and wiped my dripping nose on my sleeve. 'You realise that might be quite a lot then?' I said, trying to be funny. I rubbed my eyes and when I took my hands away he was gone.

...FADE TO BLACK

Episode Twelve

Running Through Thorns,
Crossing the Freeway and the Pink Puddle

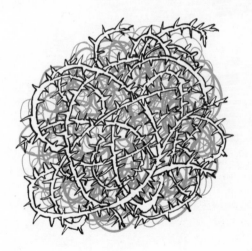

It was dark when I eventually rubbed my swollen eyes and sat up in my Malibu bedroom. Almost dark. The first blue-grey light of morning was frosting the pillow and sheets on the bed beside me and picking out the strange shapes of piles of discarded clothes and books scattered across the floor. I felt a wave of panic, like when you're in a crowded lift and the door takes a little bit too long to open on your floor. I kicked back the bed sheets. I needed to get out. I pulled on my sneakers and sweater and crept through the silent house. It was cool outside and a breeze rattled the thick leaves of the spiky shrubs around the pool. There was a rumbling sound too, just a low purr, like a cat when it's sitting on your lap. I couldn't tell if it was cars on the freeway or the sound of the ocean

. . . *the ocean.*

I began to run. I had to get to *the ocean.*

When I reached the heavy metal gate at the end of the drive, I eased open the tiny door halfway up that allowed you to see who was outside. There was no one; no journalists, no cameras, no one. I pressed the release button, the gate swung open and I closed my eyes as it clanged shut behind me. Running again, this time with my eyes half closed, I made another wish. I wished that they'd all lost interest, the press, the world, everyone, but I knew it wouldn't work. Even when my wishes came true, everything always went wrong. Just when you think you're happy, it all turns rotten. People lie to you and people die.

Ned was dead.

I ran along a road with dense trees on both sides, then found that the lane had started to climb, so I turned downhill again on to a narrow path, passing tall fences, high walls and small yards with rubbish bins – running, tumbling downhill. A small building, a shed, was emitting a low humming sound – a pool filter pump, maybe. Running downhill. I pushed past a plant that was partly blocking the path. It had vicious thorns which scratched my arms but I didn't care. I wanted it to hurt. I wanted to feel something other than the unbearable ache in my chest. I plunged through another thorn bush. I didn't care about anything any more. Nothing but running. Just keep running.

I reached a winding lane where the misty grey shapes of low buildings crouched behind the trees. I tripped and my ankle hit a big stone on the path. A sharp pain made me screw up my face but I couldn't stop. Limping now, I stumbled on, gulping in lungfuls of sharp air, until I reached the coast road.

Even this early, before dawn, there was a lot of traffic. I stood for a moment, catching my breath and watching the cars and trucks whizz by. It was barely light. I could step in front of a lorry. The driver wouldn't see me until it was too late. Then I'd be with Ned and Mum. It would all be over in a second. Less than a second. Just take a step. One step.

aarrp!

A truck was heading straight for me, hooting. I was standing in the middle of the freeway, blinded by the headlights. My body switched instantly to automatic and I jumped, like an insect, across to the other side, to safety. Adrenalin and terror made my heart hammer against my ribcage. I reached down and grabbed my knees, thinking that I might throw up, then blew out my cheeks, took some deep breaths and looked around.

High walls stretched the length of the highway, shielding the enormous luxury beach-front houses and blocking my route. I began to jog again, looking for a gap, and within just a few paces there it was, a narrow path between a restaurant and a house. I ran down the path and, at the end, it opened out on to the pale, wide sand and an endless horizon of the rolling ocean.

EXT. LONG, SANDY BEACH, MALIBU — DAY. It is dawn. There is a strong wind and it is whipping up the sand. A woman, running with a big black dog, jogs past a lifeguard's hut. The beach is almost empty. Far off in the distance a man can be seen engaged in slow, deliberate exercise movements. EMBER FURY is walking along the edge.

I stared out at the water. I could walk into the ocean, just keep walking until I floated away; away out to sea. Ned was dead. Of course he was dead. It was ridiculous! He'd died more than sixty years ago, but, to me, it wasn't the distant past. It had happened today. My throat hurt. My head ached. It was incredibly hard trying not to cry so I folded my arms, tucked my chin into my jumper and started walking along the sand. I just kept walking.

I won't bore you with everything I thought about as I walked, but let's just say that I kinda turned over in my mind what I'd done and said and the horrible things that had happened. I even thought about stupid stuff like

running away or taking lots of pills or jumping off a tall building or filling my pockets with stones and walking into the water. Dad would be happier without me. I was trouble, a problem, an embarrassment. I didn't want to be there any more, in Los Angeles, in California or on the planet.

I thought Finn breaking my heart had felt bad, but losing Ned was a gazillion times worse. My heart had barely recovered and there it was ripped out again, put in a blender and whizzed into pulp. In fact, my whole body had been chopped into little bits and fed into the spinning metal blades. I was a puddle of Ember smoothie poured on the sand for the seagulls to peck at.

The sea breeze was quite cold so I pushed my hands into my pockets. My knuckles grazed the edge of a box, a matchbox. I pulled it out and looked at it resting in the palm of my hand. I wasn't even tempted to push it open. I'd been so stupid. Fires weren't fun, they weren't beautiful, and they definitely weren't cool. Fire had killed my best friend. I raised my hand in the air, took a step and drew my arm slowly back, then jerked it forward and threw the box with all my strength.

It sailed in a high arc and plopped into the water

The sun had begun to rise and was casting long shadows. I'd stopped walking and was watching the hypnotic pulse of the ocean, back and forth, in and out. I stared at the wide, pink puddle that was gradually being dissolved into the foamy water. I was being washed away. I had just realised that I was standing knee-deep in the waves and shivering with cold when I heard someone calling. . .

far off in the distance.

A man was waving from the lifeguard's hut and the woman with the black dog I'd seen earlier was pointing towards me. Further up the beach, I could just see the flashing red and blue lights of a police car, and a strange shape was moving rapidly along the shoreline towards me. A yellow creature emerged from the shadow of the hut and bounded

across the sand, two bright eyes blazing. It was a beach buggy, a small, open-top car, and a figure was standing next to the driver, clutching the roll bar. A figure that was sort of familiar. Very familiar. It was Dad. My dad. Suddenly, I was shouting, calling out, 'Dad!'

'Em!' he yelled as the car leapt across the beach.

'Daaaad,' I sobbed, letting myself cry at last.

The buggy kicked up a spray of water and pink goo as it splashed to a halt in the Ember smoothie puddle. Dad jumped out and hugged me to his chest. I didn't want him to ever let go.

'We were so worried,' he said, 'when your bed was empty. I imagined all sorts of terrible... You could have been kidnapped or drowned or...' He stopped, pushed me away and held my arms. He looked angry. 'I was frantic! I thought you might have done... something stupid... like... Oh, Em!'

He looked at me and saw that I was crying, even though I was trying to hide behind my fringe. My insides felt like they were being ripped out all over again. Then Dad's expression changed.

'It's OK, babycakes. Don't cry,' he said, stroking my hair.

'Oh, Dad. I'm s... sorr... sorry 'bout... everything,' I snivelled.

Dad put his arms round me again and I nuzzled into his jumper. I wiped a lot of snot on it and I think it was a pretty expensive one, but he didn't seem to mind. We were both standing in the water now, shivering, our clothes soaked. We retreated up the beach a little way and the buggy driver, a lifeguard, came over with a foil blanket which he draped around us. He led us both back to the car and we climbed in.

'Tell me what happened,' said Dad.

I blurted out the whole story, right from the beginning;

everything I've just told you. Dad listened in silence, sometimes nodding, often frowning. I told him about finding myself in London during the Blitz and Ned's family eating their pet. I told him the truth about taking his car and the fake motel and the rabbit that saved our lives. I cried again, oozing gallons more snot, when I told him about Ned, the hero, saving the kids from the fire.

. . . sniff. . . 'sounds crazy, doesn't it?' I said.

Dad didn't answer. He was frowning again because he'd just noticed the red, bleeding scratches on my arms. I guess he thought I might have cut myself on purpose. I suppose I did, in a way, but I had to make him believe that the whole idea was absurd, so I laughed and explained about running through the spiky plants up the hill.

'Come on. Let's go home,' he said.

Episode Thirteen

Aftershocks

INT. LYNDON FURY'S STUDY, MALIBU — DAY. The room is eclectically furnished. There are unusual items of furniture, a couple of guitars on stands, lots of books and CDs, gold discs and photographs on the walls and a Union Jack rug on the floor. EMBER is curled up in a leather chair, wrapped in a blanket, drinking hot chocolate from a mug while she listens to a conversation outside.

I could hear Dad talking to Jerry and the cops outside. Jerry was going on about CCTV cameras and alarms not working and someone else said they wanted to call a doctor. Dad said they weren't to worry, he would deal with it. Jerry should show the police out and go and organise some breakfast. Then dad came into his study and began to pace around the room, picking up books and objects absent-mindedly. He was definitely stressed out about something.

'Em, I've got something quite important to discuss with you.' Dad rubbed his hand across his chin. He looked tired.

'I'm going to jail,' I said. Jail was what I deserved. Like Charity said, I'd done bad things and I needed to pay for them.

'Em, you're not going to jail.'

'Oh. But I thought. . .'

I put the mug of chocolate down on the edge of Dad's desk. The mug jiggled. That's so weird, I thought. The mug was jiggling across the desk, to the edge. . . and toppled over the side in a soaring dive towards the carpet. I just watched it, as if it was all in *s l o w - m o t i o n .*

I looked up at Dad.

'Em, get up!' he shouted.

'What?' I said, confused. I glanced back down at the mug, lying on the rug in a chocolate puddle, still jiggling. Wait, the floor was jiggling. My chair was jiggling.

'Earthquake!' said Dad. 'Get under the desk!'

I stood up and Dad grabbed my arm. His face was grey so it wasn't a joke. The door crashed open and Jerry, panting and sweaty, stood there with his arms braced against the sides of the frame.

'Earthquake!' he shouted.

'We know!' Dad and I said in unison, from under the desk.

The whole house felt as if it had been put on a tray of sand and someone was shaking it backwards and forwards. A couple of books hit the rug behind me and a framed photo smashed against a shelf on its way down. It was like being back in the air-raid shelter.

And then it stopped

And then it stopped. And then it stopped. And then it stopped. And then it stopped.

I felt sick and looked up at Jerry, who was still in the doorway. I wanted to ask him if it was over but was unable to speak.

'It's OK,' he said reassuringly. 'It was just a small one.'

I released my grip on Dad's arm. My knuckles had gone white and his jumper was creased into a shrivelled knot where I'd held it.

Dad got up, he and Jerry rushed out and suddenly I was alone in an empty, silent room. That was so weird, I thought. What just happened? I couldn't work out what was real any more, like when I was standing outside that burned-out house in London, after the fire. Was it all my imagination? Had those crazy things really happened to me? Setting fire to a fake motel, falling in love with a phoney boyfriend, crying over my dead, imaginary friend. Was that an earthquake or just Hollywood special effects? I felt like someone had just flicked the switch on the blender. I was whizzed into a bewildered pulp again.

I don't know exactly what happened to me that morning, under the desk; what changed. The only way I can explain it is that someone scooped up the gloopy Ember puddle, shook it up and poured it into a me-shaped mould. When it was set, a new me came out. I still felt like I'd been liquidised, but somehow I was the new edition, the latest, improved Ember download, the updated, rebooted, Version 2.0. Does that sound dumb?

'Em, there may be aftershocks, so stay under the desk.' Dad was calling from somewhere. I think he was outside in the garden. I'd already uncurled myself from the floor and New Ember sat back in the chair. I had ignored Dad's instruction to stay under the desk, you see, because I'd decided it was probably all make-believe. And even if it wasn't and everything was real, then I had to deal with it. I pulled the blanket round me. I needed to get my head straight.

Dad had been about to say something really important.

This was serious.

What could have made him look so upset?

Was he dying of a fatal illness?

Had he lost all his money playing on-line poker?

Was he really a CIA hit man pretending to be a rock star?

It was like waiting to be executed.

New Ember prepared herself for horrible news.

'We've had quite a day, haven't we, Em?' Dad said. He was sitting on the leather sofa, leaning forward with his elbows on his knees. I'd been waiting almost an hour for him to check the house for damage. They'd found nothing but a single tiny crack in a wall in the garden and there had been no aftershocks.

Yet.

'How would you feel about going back to London. . . with me. . . to Orchard Farm?'

'With you?' I asked, puzzled. I hadn't expected that.

'Charity's right. It's about time I started being a proper dad.' He took a deep breath. 'All that stuff,' he pointed at the pile of newspapers and magazines on his desk, 'well, it's true, isn't it? Absent father. Unfit parent.'

'But I'm the one who stole your car, set fire to the motel. . . ran away.'

Dad got up and began to pace around the room.

'I know I was never very good at the dad stuff, but I'm gonna change all that. I've told the band I need to spend more time with you and I'm not going to tour any more.' He sighed. 'Your mum always knew what to do. Do you remember the time you scalped your dolls?'

I did remember. I was about three or four, I think. I was annoyed that mum was busy, or something, and I was fed up and I'd decided to see what my favourite doll would look like without her yellow ponytail. I had to move a heavy chair so I could climb up to reach some scissors in the kitchen, then I just went snip, snip, snip. The doll looked horrible without hair, ugly and scary, but I returned to my room and gave the same treatment to all the others. Every one of my dolls got an extreme haircut.

'Your mum said you didn't deserve to have toys and she put them in rubbish bags, said she'd take them to children who would treat them properly, d'you remember?'

Mum must have told Dad the story, I thought, because I didn't recall him being there at the time. Perhaps he was. Maybe he had been upstairs packing for another tour.

'I lay on the floor, screaming my head off,' I said. 'Mum told me all I had to do to get them back was to say I was sorry. I wouldn't say it. . . I lay on the floor for ages.' I paused, remembering. 'Later, when she hugged me for apologising, she had blue paint in her hair. . . I found one of her paintings.'

'Your mum's?' said Dad, still walking backwards and forwards. I wished he would sit down.

'Yeah, in a gallery here in L.A. A really tiny one of a heart and a key.'

Dad stopped, stood still and frowned. Something had occurred to him.

'Your present,' he said.

'What?' I said, pretending not to be interested. I had heard him perfectly well, but didn't want to sound too eager.

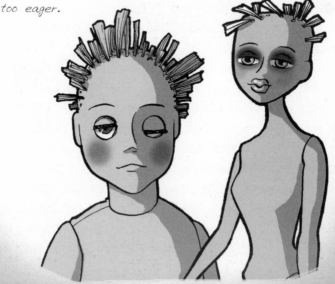

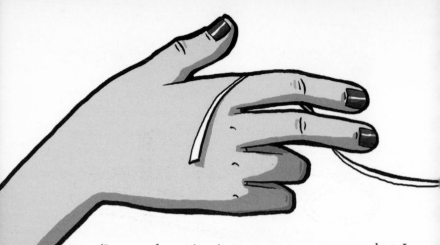

'I wanted to give it to you at your party, but I missed it. Sorry 'bout that. Here,' he said, and took a small blue box from a drawer in the desk and handed it to me. It was really light and I tried not to look disappointed. I untied the white ribbon and eased off the lid. Inside, under several layers of tissue paper, was a shiny oval on a chain, a bit like a thick coin, but with curved edges. It was pale gold and painted all over with tiny blue flowers. Across the centre was a painted pale blue ribbon with the words *Forget Me Not* written on it.

'It was your mum's,' said Dad, his voice choking a bit. 'It's a locket. Look inside.'

I noticed a small indentation on one edge and carefully pushed at it with my fingernail. The locket opened like a shell to reveal two photographs, one in each side. On the left was a picture of Dad that I hadn't seen before. He had his head thrown back and was laughing at what must have been a hilarious joke, or something. On the other side was a beautiful woman, smiling and holding her hair back, the way I do sometimes, with both her palms flat on the top of her head. It was mum. Gradually she went out of focus as my eyes filled with water. I sniffed and wiped my nose on the back of my hand.

'Dad. . . it's awesome. Thanks,' I said.

'Your mum told me a long time ago that she wanted you to have it. But I forgot all about it until it came in a box of stuff that was sent from London. I put the picture of me in it.' He went all quiet and thoughtful for a moment.

'What would I want a picture of you for?' I said, laughing and punching him on the arm.

'Hey, a few years ago, every teenager would have had a picture of me on their bedroom wall.' He licked his finger and swept it over his eyebrow with an exaggerated swish.

'I know,' I said, giggling, and remembering that Finn was one of them.

'I've got something else,' he said, taking a second, bigger package, wrapped in blue paper, from a shelf. It looked and felt like a book.

'What is it?' I said. Duh! I knew what it was.

'I know you've read it, but it's. . . well, open it and you'll see what I mean.'

I ripped the blue paper and *Alice's Adventures in Wonderland* dropped into my lap. It had an embossed green fabric cover and smelled slightly of dust and libraries.

'It's not a first edition but it's quite old and I know you love the illustrations.'

'Wow!' I just grinned, then leaned over and kissed him on his stubbly cheek. The book was almost as perfect as the locket.

Episode Fourteen

Family Day, The Brilliant Idea
and Mikko Drives a Ferrari

INT. HEATHROW AIRPORT, LONDON — DAY. Flashbulbs and bright TV lights dazzle EMBER and LYNDON as they emerge into the arrivals hall and are greeted by jostling photographers and TV cameras.

The airport was chaotic. One journalist called out, 'Why d'ya come back here, Lyndon? Is your marriage over? Where's your wife?'

Dad got really angry and pushed the guy out of the way. Then, with enormous relief, we saw a security guard and a couple of policemen forcing people back and we managed to get out of the terminal and into a waiting car. We weren't quite quick enough though, because, as the door closed, I heard someone shouting, 'Hey, Ember. You here to find another school to burn down? Need a light?'

'Scum!' Dad yelled, as we tumbled on to the back seat. His face was red and he looked quite angry, but then it sort of crumpled into a smile and he started laughing.

'Need a light? That's quite funny,' I said, getting the giggles.

'Yeah. Real comedians, those journalists. . . ha ha ha. . .'

We both laughed until our stomachs hurt, then sat quietly for a bit, getting our breath back. Neither of us said anything for ages as the traffic gradually became slower and slower the further we got into London. Eventually, I couldn't hold it in any longer.

'Dad?'

'Mmm?'

'Charity hasn't left you, has she?'

'She's taking a bit of time away. Her new film is quite important.'

'More important than you?'

'That's not what I mean.'

'I heard you,' I said. 'I heard you arguing in L.A. and I heard what Charity said about me. She left because of me, didn't she? Because of what I did.'

'No, Em. It's not your fault.'

'I was horrible to her.'

Dad frowned and looked out of the window.

'Yes, you were.'

INT. LUXURY HOTEL SUITE, LONDON — DAY. The hotel room is fabulous. EMBER and LYNDON each have their own enormous bedroom separated by a lounge the size of a small house. EMBER's room is very chic with its own marble bathroom and circular bath. CLOSE-UP: EMBER pulls back the sheer curtains on the window and looks out across the rooftops of London.

We were home. I had a big lump in my throat and my chest felt like I was wearing one of those corset things and someone was pulling it tighter and tighter. I'd really missed the grey, damp city. . . and my friends. . . and Ned.

---

account   privacy   logout

my page

Ember Fury. . .

alias: flamegrrl
loves: my dad
hates: british journalists
my fave city: london (my hometown)
my fave food: anything from room service
my fave movie: donnie darko

what I'm doing today. . .

listening:
blur
the jam
the kinks

reading:
neverwhere – neil gaiman alice's adventures in wonderland – lewis carroll (from my dad)

today's chat:

flamegrrl: u hear about my adventure?

mk: the whole planet knows what you did

dazed: finn's blog is hottest on the planet did u really run away with him?

flamegrrl: don't mention the f word!!! h8 him!!!

dazed: duz ruby have spots? wots she like?

flamegrrl: freaky – like crayon drawing by your baby sister

mk: u really going back to the farm?

flamegrrl: woz farm or prison this time

mk: i bet that's not true you liar

flamegrrl: puppies

post reply

EXT. ORCHARD FARM — DAY. A silver-grey limousine sweeps up the gravel drive, past stables and tennis courts, and stops outside a large redbrick Victorian farmhouse. A painted wooden sign in the flowerbed by the front door says, 'Welcome to Orchard Farm'.

It was Saturday, 'Family Day' at the Farm, so there were lots of people in the garden and sitting on the sunny terrace, which is where we had a cup of tea with Dr Redmond. The lawyers and my social workers had made their decision: I had to be 're-assessed' at the Farm and this time dad must come too. I might have to check in for another eight weeks, if that was Dr Redmond's recommendation.

Dr Redmond asked lots of questions; the types of questions that you know are really a sort of test. I said I was starting to understand the consequences of my actions, because dad and I had agreed in the car that this would be a good thing to say. Then dad said the other thing we'd talked about in the car: that he was learning to be a better father. I told her some of the stuff that happened in L.A. and dad kept looking at me because he knew the bits I was leaving out. She asked about why I kept running away and about the times when I got really angry. I said that I didn't feel so angry any more and she nodded and wrote something down. It seemed to be going quite well, but we were still both surprised at the end when Dr Redmond said what she was going to put in her report. We would both have to attend family sessions once a month, but she thought that the best thing would be for me and Dad to spend time getting to know each other. That was it!

Before we left, Dr Redmond had another surprise. She'd decided to set me a task.

'Would you like to do something to remember your mum,

Ember?' she said. 'Perhaps you could do some drawings, like the lovely ones you did in Art Therapy. Or it could be a poem or a photograph album. Your dad could help.'

I decided exactly what I was going to do on the way back to London and I thought it was a brilliant idea.

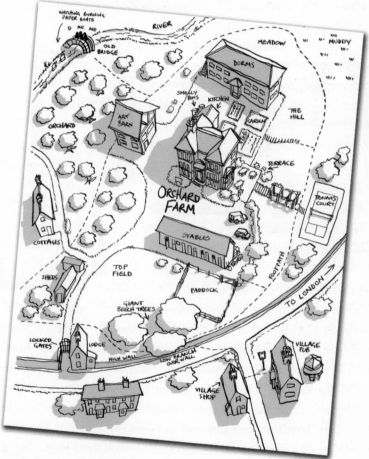

Dad thought an exhibition
of Mum's paintings was a brilliant idea too and as soon as we started planning it the project just seemed to get bigger and bigger. 'What about a book?' and 'How about a documentary?'

Suddenly we had a whole 'media event' on our hands. It was fantastic! Dad and I were really busy every day, dashing around London, hiring a publicist, going to meetings and interviews and looking at venues. It was amazing being with Dad all the time but I soon discovered that he was kinda reluctant to let me out of his sight. I think all the stupid stuff I did in California had made him a bit paranoid.

I got a text from Daze,

I replied,

wht hppnd @ frm?
D x

Reply   Options   Menu

im free!
need 2 c u
EM x

Send   Options   Menu

hrd 2 escp
wtchd 24/7
D x

Reply

u thnk of smthng
u + mk our spcl
plc thrs @ 4
EM x

Send   Options   Menu

I decided I had to get away from Dad, just for a few hours, so I texted back,

I didn't have time to think about Ned.

It wasn't until one afternoon, when Dad and I were in a taxi in south London, that I remembered the last time I'd been in that part of the city. We were travelling back to the hotel from a photographer's studio. The studio was above a pub in Clapham. We had to go through the bar, out the back and up a clanging metal staircase that reminded me of the fire escape at Club Fahrenheit. The noise of our feet on the steps gave me a little bit of a shiver, like someone had scratched their finger down the back of my T-shirt. We pushed open an old door at the top into an enormous white room. It was like the whole attic of the building had been cleaned out and sprayed white. It couldn't have been more different from the bar downstairs or the rundown street outside. We were there to have our portraits taken by this cool fashion photographer, but he turned out to be much older and a lot less cool than I thought. It was really boring, too. I got fed up posing. The photographer kept saying things like 'smile, tilt your head. . . look at your dad. . . yeah, that's great. . . awesome. . .' He was so fake.

On the way back, the session over, we drove past Clapham Common and that's when I remembered Ned. I wished he was still around. Having my photo taken would have been much more fun with Ned making jokes about the photographer's jeans being too tight and his dyed blond hair with its disgusting dark roots.

I was just wondering if I would ever see Ned again, and feeling incredibly sad, when the sound of Dad's mobile ringtone filled the taxi (a stupid Blondie song about telephones, which he thought was funny). He pulled the phone out of his pocket, slid it open with a click and put it to his ear.

'OK, sounds great,' he said. 'Can we take a look tomorrow? Yeah. Eleven is fine. OK. Bye.'

He closed the phone, looked at me and smiled.

'What's the stupid grin for?' I asked.

'I think I might have found the perfect place. But you have to see it.'

'What do you mean?' I asked. 'You don't mean the venue for the exhibition? I thought that was decided.'

'No, not the gallery. A house.'

'Whose house?'

'Our house?'

The house was in a tree-lined street in west London where we were greeted by a red-faced estate agent. It was raining so we ran up a crunching gravel drive and climbed wide stone steps into a beautiful old white building, half covered by a creeper trailing leaves and tiny, dripping, white flowers. As we walked from one empty room to another I began to imagine curling up on a sofa here, making a sandwich for Dad in there, sitting and sketching on that window seat. I wanted it to be my home so much it hurt.

'What do you think?' Dad asked.

'I love it,' I exclaimed.

'How would you feel if we stayed in London?'

'You mean me, live with you, here?' I said.

'Yeah.'

'I'd love it,' I said, trying not to sound too excited.

'I know you want to go to art college, so if we find you a school and you do your exams in a couple of years, you could apply to some colleges in London. What do you think?'

'Oh, Dad!' I said, unable to hold back any longer. 'You were so wrong, you know, about all the dad stuff. You're the best!'

On Thursday afternoon, while Dad was on the phone, I sneaked out of the hotel room, took the lift down to the lobby and walked out on to a drizzly, noisy street. I felt bad about sneaking out, so I'd left him a note. I thought Dad might panic like last time, think I'd done something 'stupid' and call the police. He hadn't let me out of his sight for almost two weeks and I was desperate to get out.

I had a date.

INT. SOHO COFFEE BAR — DAY. The café is busy with a mix of customers, young and old, tourists and workers.

It was raining really hard by the time I got to the Target Café, our café, our special meeting place. I hadn't brought a coat or umbrella or anything and I'd got

really wet. Daze and Mikko were already there, grinning at me from our usual table in the corner. We had this big cheesy hug and then it was like an explosion, or when a dam collapses in a movie, flooding whole villages. We emptied out everything that had happened since we'd last been together. I told my L.A. story although, of course, they knew some of it from the gossip mags. I just left out some stuff about Finn. . . and Ned.

Daze asked lots of questions about Finn and I tried to change the subject.

'Dad got dumped,' I said, knowing Daze would probably be far more interested in Charity than in Finn the Fake.

'Not really dumped,' said Daze. 'She's only moved out temporarily.'

'How do you know that?' I asked, amazed.

'I check the Hollywood websites every day. I can't believe Charity Lane is your stepmum, Em. She's so beautiful. How does she stay so thin? Does she have a personal trainer?' Then Daze moaned about her 'house arrest' and being watched all the time by her parents and forced to eat chips and pasta and milkshakes four times a day.

Mikko had the opposite situation. He was staying with his aunt because she lived close to his new college. His aunt let him do whatever he wanted.

'No plans to impersonate the Prime Minister or break into Buckingham Palace, then?' I asked him.

'Nah! Thought I'd conserve my energy for a bit. I *am* gonna test drive a Ferrari this afternoon, though,' he said, stretching and putting his hands behind his head. He lifted his damp sneakers on to a chair at the next table.

'You're not old enough. . . and you haven't got a licence,' said Daze, exasperated. Then she smiled and said, 'Can I come?'

A smart-looking old lady came into the café, shook out

her big black umbrella and spotted the empty table behind us. When she reached our table, in her journey through the room, she stopped. Mikko's legs were blocking her path.

'Excuse me, young man,' she said with a really posh accent. 'Would you mind moving your boots?' She was elegant and quite pretty. . . for an old woman.

'I remember the war, don't you know,' said Mikko, mimicking her accent and dropping his feet noisily to the floor. 'In my day we wouldn't have tolerated such behaviour.'

'Don't make jokes about the war,' I said angrily. 'You don't know what it was like, not knowing if you'd be alive the next day. You've no idea how it feels to be hungry and scared all the time.'

Daze and Mikko were staring at me with their mouths open. I think I must've been shouting because the café had gone quiet and people were looking at me. Their faces were saying, watch out for the mad teenager, she may bite!

'Sorry,' I said, feeling my face going really hot and red. The old lady sat down. I could see a twinkle in her eye and the smallest hint of a smile twitched briefly on her lips. She looked ever so slightly like Ned's sister Jane.

'Puppies!' said Daze.

Episode Fifteen

Spitting Crab Salad, Trying on Hats
and Finally Getting It

The week that the 'Amica' exhibition opened, the publicity was everywhere – posters on buses, articles in newspapers and even a mention on the TV news. A short documentary about Mum and Dad was aired on this trendy arts programme. It was the first time I'd seen some of the cheesy romantic stuff about how Mum and Dad got together. It was also the first time I'd looked at Mum's paintings properly. Dad and I had surfed the Net searching for them all over the world, so I'd mostly seen them as tiny pictures on a screen. We'd asked all the different galleries and private collectors if we could borrow them for the exhibition and some of them had arrived in our hotel room, but covered in paper or bubble wrap. I didn't get a peek before they were sent on to the gallery.

Every channel ran Dad's interview. I guess you saw it. I hated the clip they showed over and over, where Dad had tears in his eyes. Serious puppies! Dad said it was all out of context and edited for 'emotional effect', but it was all good publicity and that was the important thing.

We were having a Private View for friends and press on Thursday night and I invited Daze and Mikko as my guests. Lots of journalists and news cameras would be there and celebrities were flying in from all over the world.

Dad made his evil request over lunch at The Ivy. He said he wanted me to wear a *dress*! Aaarrgh! I almost spat out my crab salad. He said he was sick of seeing me in skinny jeans and sneakers, so he'd hired a stylist. My own stylist! She was really nice, actually. She came to the hotel and had all these cool things sent over from some designers. Then she said that one of the big stores would open that night just for us. I'd read somewhere that only huge celebrities get that sort of treatment, so it was completely mind-blowing. I asked if I could take a friend.

cn u cm
shppng?
EM x

ys bt wot do i tll
olds + whts opn @
10.08pm!? D x

ul c
pk u up in 20
EM x

Stylist

It was kinda like being in a cake shop and being allowed to taste a bit of everything – iced buns, jam doughnuts, fairy cakes, strawberry tarts and chocolate fudge cake, all hanging on rails. We tried on embroidered coats, gold leather jackets, satin suits, flared purple trousers, denim miniskirts, frilly blouses, short sequinned dresses, long chiffon dresses, high-heeled boots, beaded sandals, feather capes, even hats. I couldn't believe that I was actually enjoying trying on clothes! In the end I chose a simple black dress and flat shoes. Daze was infuriated with me but agreed that the dress was the only thing that really looked right. The stylist said someone would come to do my hair and make-up. I would wear only one piece of jewellery – Mum's locket.

EXT. GALLERY, LONDON — DAY. It's late summer and early evening. The sun is low in the sky and there's a golden glow bathing the city. The street is full of people. There are heaving crowds of fans, photographers with lights flashing, and film crews, all pressed behind barriers.

Arriving at the gallery was thrilling. It was the coolest event of the end of summer. Dad held my hand as we walked from the limousine. We smiled and waved.

'It's great to be back in London, thank you for coming,' Dad said, about a million times, to every journalist, whatever their shouted question, all the way up to the entrance. Inside was a bit quieter, but there were photographers there too. Dad's PR woman guided everyone through the room and out into a sort of garden at the back where there was a marquee and tables stacked with the glossy exhibition catalogue – *AMICA*. Waiters were floating about with shimmering trays of champagne. I spotted Daze and Mikko, who had helped themselves to a glass each and were standing on the grass. Daze looked amazing. She was wearing this gorgeous dress with flowers all over it, very high platform shoes and bright red lipstick. She could have passed for twenty-four instead of fourteen. No wonder nobody stopped her from drinking the champagne. Dad began an interview with a woman in a yellow suit, a TV camera right in his face, so I was able to slip away. I ran across the lawn to my friends.

Mikko was wearing shades, a cool, dark grey suit, a white shirt and a narrow black tie. I could tell there was a reason he'd put so much thought into his appearance. He was pretending to be someone else.

'Ciao, bambina!' he said as I approached, and air-kissed me on either side of my face, like he was some Euro-trash fashion

celeb or something. 'Scuse me. I'm going to mingle.' He marched across the garden and into the gallery.

Daze gave me a hug. 'Isn't this amazing?' she said, sipping her champagne. 'You look lovely. How do you feel? Are you OK? I expect you want a bit of time on your own to look at the exhibition, don't you?'

Daze always seemed to know exactly what I was thinking. 'Yeah. Do you mind?' I said. 'I'll come and find you later, I promise.'

No one noticed when I took a glass of champagne too and swallowed it down in about three, bubbling gulps. No one noticed because something else was the centre of attention – Mum's pictures and my dad talking about them. I put my empty glass back on a tray and went into the gallery.

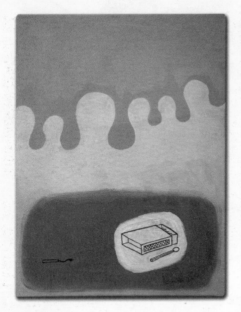

The space was perfect for Mum's paintings.

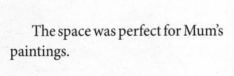

There were three white high-ceilinged rooms, one leading into another. The pictures were all different sizes but similar in style – simple flat colours, egg shapes, boxes, rectangles,

blobs, marks and wobbly outlines. Some were sort of abstract but in others you could see the shapes of places or people or objects. Familiar places. Familiar people.

I saw the sunset painting as soon as
I stepped into the last room. It was
straight opposite, under a skylight, and
the colours glowed – yellow, orange,
purple and deep blue. The subject was
like all the others, strangely familiar. Very
familiar. The canvas was huge, taller than

me, filling the wall. It was a vast landscape. Although it was really just coloured shapes, somehow you could see the golden clouds burning in a vivid sky above towering rocks and, in the corner, a little group of figures. . . watching. There were three people, holding hands, but a fourth shape sat beside them. A tiny smudge of white paint. A creature with long ears and a turned-up nose. . . a rabbit.

I clutched the front of my dress in shock and the locket fell, hit the floor and popped open. I slid to my knees, on to the slippery wooden boards, and scooped it up, afraid that I might have damaged it. The photo of Mum had fallen out and was lying face down. There was something written on the back in tiny blue ballpoint, letters. I held it up and read,

Out of the corner of my eye, I saw Daze and Mikko standing together in the doorway. Daze was about to run towards me, but Mikko held her back. He said something to her and she looked over. I held up my hand and smiled to say that I was OK. I needed some time to think.

I know that you are screaming at me right now. You probably worked it all out pages ago. But it wasn't until that moment that everything seemed to fall into place. I sat on the floor staring at the locket. I was really confused and my head was spinning but it was starting to make a sort of crazy sense, to fit together in a freaky way. Mum's message in the locket reminded me of what Ned said before he went away. He said he'd be keeping an eye on me, any time I felt like setting fire to something. Had Mum wanted me to know that, even though she was gone, like Ned, she was still watching over me. . . keeping me safe?

Then there were the paintings. The paintings were mind-blowing. It was as if Mum had done them all for me. More than that, they seemed to be about me. But how could they be? Was I seeing something in them that wasn't there or had Mum been there 'with me' in the diner, at Club Fahrenheit, in the desert, on the beach?

I sat there staring at the sunset painting for ages, while people wandered through the room and filled it with loud chatter. No one paid any attention to me, even though I was still sitting on the floor. I was trying to get my head straight, and something else had occurred to me. Poor Ned. Perhaps he hadn't been my imaginary friend because I needed him, or anything like that. Maybe visiting me was how he got away from all the terrible things in the Blitz – the fires and the bombs and the people dying. Just like when I'd found myself with him in London when I couldn't stand being in L.A.

And Mum did it too. Mum could escape from her life when she needed to and the paintings proved it.

The room was almost empty. People had wandered into the other rooms. I stood up and held out my hand to touch the rough paint of the sunset picture.

'Hi, Mum. I got your message,' I whispered.

I paused, thought for a moment and coughed nervously. I'd sounded really dumb, like I was leaving a voicemail, so I started again.

'I think I kinda understand, Mum, the locket and the paintings and everything. I'm sorry I caused so much trouble. I was horrible to Dad. . . and Charity. Dad loves her, you know. Not as much as he loved you, of course, but I know he wants her to come back. If she does, I'm going to try really hard to be friends with her. I promise. . . and Mum, I forgive you for leaving me. I know it was really hard for you. . .'

I had to stop because there was a lot of noise at the other end of the gallery. Everyone seemed to have rushed to the entrance and there were photographers calling out to someone who'd just arrived.

'Charity, over here!' someone yelled.

The stepmom has landed, I thought. I rubbed my wet cheek, hoping my mascara hadn't run.

A scrum of people, a sort of dense cloud of raised voices and flashing lights, moved slowly through the room, and as they reached a bench in the middle they parted like a curtain revealing Dad and Charity, standing close together, holding hands.

'Miss Lane, why are you in London?' asked a journalist.

'To support my husband,' said Charity, neon smile flashing.

'Charity, how do you feel about what your husband has been doing over here?' asked a woman TV reporter, thrusting a microphone at her.

'I'm very proud of him.'

'What about the stories about you falling out with your stepdaughter?'

Charity looked straight at the reporter.

'We didn't fall out,' she said. 'It wasn't easy for her in L.A. Can you imagine spending your teens in the spotlight, being a rock star's daughter?' Everyone laughed. 'Ember is an exceptional young woman. It's a privilege being her stepmom. I can't wait to get to know her better.'

'What are you going to do now?'

Charity looked at Dad and he nodded.

'I'm moving to London.'

Her performance was perfect. Another Oscar-winner.

A roar of questions erupted, so that you couldn't hear anyone speaking any more. Charity and Dad both saw me through the crowd and waved. Then they turned to each other and kissed. It was like the kiss at the end of a really cheesy movie, only this kiss was drowned in a wave of babbling voices and paparazzi flash bulbs. Nobody could have written a better happy ending, could they?

I walked out of the gallery on to the lawn and found a quiet spot to sit and take it all in. Waiters were clearing champagne glasses from tables, and as one of them passed me with a tray something fell off it on to the grass. I reached down and picked it up. It was a box of matches, flat and oblong, pink and white, a sort of gingham check, and there was a picture on it. It was a drawing of a rabbit. I pushed the box open with my finger, pulled out a match, and ran it along the side.

Fizzzzz. . . crack. . . whoosh. . .

It burst into life and flickered in the breeze. Then it suddenly went out. I jumped and looked behind me because I was sure I heard someone sigh.

'Ned, is that you?'

My hand shook as I took a second match out of the box. I struck it and gazed at the flame, then, whoosh! It blew out again. This time I felt the warm breath on my hand.

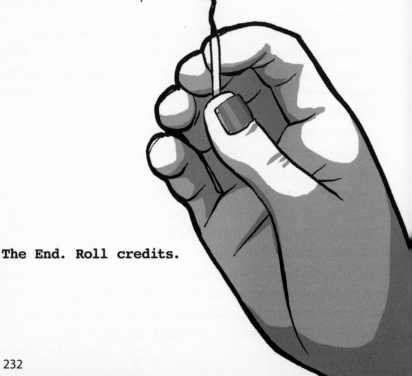

The End. Roll credits.

Introducing Scarlett...

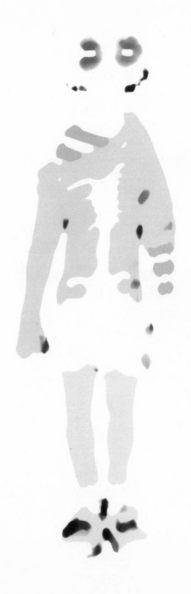

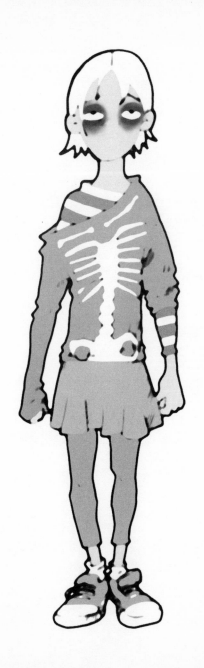

...she's dead

SCARLETT DEDD by Cathy Brett

Coming summer 2010

Ever wondered what you'd look like as an illustrated character?

Well here's your chance to find out. . .

Visit www.emberfury.co.uk and check out the blog to find out how to win a part in SCARLETT DEDD, Cathy Brett's next book!